HOUSE OF DOORS
by Nicholas Fletcher

House of Doors

Copyright © 2020 Nicholas Fletcher

Front cover based on photo by Linford Miles (on Unsplash).

Rear cover based on photo by Lillian Grace (on Unsplash).

Covers edited by Kendall Fletcher (lostximagination on Tumblr).

Chapter 1 Illustration of Alexis by K. Aversari (WinterPolarBear

on deviantart/polaratelier.carrd.co)

Chapter 3 Illustration of Alice by Kendall Fletcher

(lostximagination on Tumblr).

CHAPTER 1

Light cracks through the gap in the curtains on my window, shining into my eyes and… it's raining… *again.*

Hopping out of bed and looking around the house, I see there's a note on the counter. It seems that Dad's gone off to the beach for the weekend and left me here.

Hm. Good. How kind of him.

Think he left anything in the kitchen today?

… That's a no. *Well.* Off to the store it is, then.

First thing, I round up the cash stored all over the house. Pausing at one particular stash, I tilt my head to the side. Is this one his or mine… you know, *whatever*, he doesn't care, why should I? It's *mine* now.

Before I head out, I probably *should* make sure I don't look totally horrid today, or at least that I look like a girl.

Popping off to the bathroom, I inspect myself in the mirror. My hair is *bad* today. The brown roots are showing again; I need to get some black dye while at the store. Whatever, just brush it flat down my back and be done with it.

Slipping off my plain black t-shirt, I slip on an adaptable bra and adjust the padding before picking the shirt back up from the floor and putting in on. This shirt is

good for me; doesn't hug too tight over my chest... I should probably put on some proper pants though.

Catching myself staring in my own pitch-black eyes and pasty skin, I quickly snap my gaze away. No sense dwelling beyond what I can address now; if I start doing this now, I won't stop for hours. I just swap my pants for a pair of old jeans, and grab a jacket before going out the door.

Walking to the store, there's a strangely strong wind blowing, immediately messing up my hair, making my brushing of it rather moot.

Forging through the wind and rain, I get to the store, and do my shopping as quickly as possible, and then drop them off at the house, hiding the bags in my room where he can't find them.

After a couple donuts, it's time to stop by the pharmacy before Guy goes to break; everyone else there asks too many questions like "Who are you?" and "What do you want?".

I should learn his name one of these days, but then I'd have to read his nametag, and that takes *effort*.

The wind is getting worse... maybe I should have got the food at the pharmacy to save a trip. This seems to quickly be turning into a storm.

The winds sound like... a whispering voice. What's it saying?

"Ta sa la."

... So nothing then. Clearly, I need to add an antipsychotic to the cocktail; that will mix well with the sertraline and the estrogen and... whatever else it is they put in there.

I just need to walk in, get my drugs, and get out. Hopefully no one tries to talk to me today; the wind's conversation is enough.

The moment I go in, I spot Guy back at the counter; right where he's supposed to be. He always sticks out, with his bright clothes against his dark brown skin- like the opposite of me.

7

I'm glad he's here- and that I know his schedule so well. If he wasn't, I'd have to come back later. Hurrying back to him, I wordlessly hand him my ID- the real one, not the other one- and the cash to get my meds and leave.

... He added a heart shaped cookie to my bag. Hm. Thanks, I guess. I'll eat it on the way home.

Just as I'm reaching the house, a burst of wind takes me up off my feet and over the old fence around the house next door. *What the fuck*!? I knew I was skinny but I'm not *that* light?!

Standing up, I brush myself off, and glance at the house I landed next to.This house has been here forever; I've never seen anyone in it before. Honestly, it's a surprise the place hasn't fallen over.

Well, with *this* wind, I give it an hour.

"Enter." The winds hiss around me.

Great. The wind is talking again... and this time it wants me to break into an abandoned house. *I don't think so.*

Returning home and taking my meds, I start to check the internet when my phone rings. It's Alice, my shrink. She's... she's got a good heart, but she's overbearing.

"Yeah." I say, answering the phone.

"Hello, Alexis. You doing alright?" Of course she's calling to check on me.

"Yeah, everything's fine."

"Good. Take your pills?"

"Just took them." Like always; why does she insist on asking?

"Perfect. I heard there's some crazy wind down there today."

"Yeah, they pushed me around a bit, but it will take more than that to stop me."

"Huh." She pauses for a moment; I hear her moving her phone. "Can I talk to your dad?"

"He's not here right now."

"Know when he's coming back?"

"Monday, I think."

"So, you're home alone. Do I need to come check on you?"

"No no no no no no no, you don't need to do that; I'm fine. There's no need for you to come over."

"You sure?"

"I told you, everything is fine. He just went to the beach without me, which is fine."

"Is that you talking or is it-"

"I said it's fine; I wouldn't want to go anyway. I prefer it alone, really..."

"Alright, if you say so." She sounds less than certain.

"Bye."

"See you Thursday."

"See you then. Bye." I hang up quickly.

So, back to the internet then. I'm sure something funny has happened today; a good laugh would do me some good.

A few hours later, someone knocks on the door. Rushing over, I grab my package before even looking at it; it's about time it got here. Ripping it open, I pull out my new shirts and toss one of them on; it's a copy of Shawn's shirt from his cartoon, Shaun Galaxy. I should go show it off. Maybe that would be good... maybe I shouldn't... No, I'm doing it.

Stepping outside, the winds seem to have calmed down a bit... until I walk past that house again, when the winds flare to send me back over the fence again.

9

Okay, that's not normal; *something* is happening here. Alright wind, I'll break into the house.

Fine. I'm doing this now. I'm opening the, for some reason unlocked, door.

CHAPTER 2

The room inside seems much nicer than the space outside; it's kinda hard to believe this is inside that run-down house.

There's a nice warmth sweeping through the room. *None* of the damage outside is visible in here. It's really like a completely different place.

The room is quite small, with only one exit. Stepping through it, I find a hallway leading to a grand entryway *far* larger than the building I entered...

I don't know what's going on, but it's definitely cool.

There is a master door at the... well, it's to my left but it's clearly meant to be the front door. It's got a message engraved in it.

"To those who are lost and seek to find

a way to leave their past behind:

your search is done, so have no fear;

the door is always open here.

The House of Doors"

Well, *that's* dramatic. It sounds... inviting though, I guess. Maybe I'll... look around some more. Though, I'm starting to get a bit hungry; I really should have eaten earlier.

Slipping down a side hallway, I find a door that opens to a large dining hall. The smell of fresh food comes to me, and my stomach growls in response.

And yeah, the table is full of warm fresh seeming food, and no one is in sight.

"Is anyone there?" I don't get a response. "I'm going to have some of this, if you don't mind."

I start eating some of the food, which turns out to be *really* good. Suddenly, someone else enters the room. Oh crap...

"Um... this isn't what it looks like."

"It looks like you enjoying your meal."

Huh?

"Yeah, that... this isn't actually mine, I just found it here."

"You're new to the House, aren't you?"

"Is this a thing to be new to?"

"Yeah. I guess the House picked me to orient you; of course it did... You can keep eating; the House made this meal for you."

"The house made it? How does a building cook?" I'm thinking I've managed to walk into something more insane than I am, though the building being bigger on the inside should have tipped me off.

"This place, the House of Doors, is... I wouldn't say alive, exactly, but it thinks and does things. The rooms shift to help those who need it."

"How did I even get here? There is no way this place is in-" He cuts me off before I can get into my point.

"Let me guess. An old, abandoned building? An obscure door tucked away in a room everyone has forgotten? Or something rarer, like an arch in a decayed hedge maze?" He pauses to breathe. He's talking rather fast; it sounds like he wants to get this over with. "The House watches the world for those who belong here and opens a Door to let them in. In here, you are safe from the world. Also, you can - and should - explore the secrets of the House; some of its power can become yours."

As I open my mouth to ask who this is, something strange happens. A piece of bread from the table lifts itself from the table and into this guy's hand. I just stare for a moment.

"Excuse me, did that just-"

"Oh yes, that. That's an example of the secrets hiding within this House. This House is a deeply magical place. It gathers people here to help them and protect them. Within this house, you can make new friends and learn new skills."

"But-" As I start to object, he interrupts me again.

"One of those skills - really several skills, but let's not go there right now - one of those skills- and the most prominent of them, in fact- is magic. Just go to the library."

"The library?"

"Just go looking for it. The House will help you find it. Now, if you'll excuse me, I think that should satisfy the house and I need to go. Good luck."

And he's gone... and he says I can learn magic in the library. Well, I have to check this out. But first, I'm eating this food. It's too good and I'm too hungry to leave all of it sit here.

After the meal is done, I go looking for the library... which is right down the hallway and around a corner. The shelves seem to go on forever. But I just need to know where to start. Suddenly, a book falls off a nearby shelf. Picking it up, I thumb through the start. It appears to be a basic starting book. Exactly what I needed. Thanks... house? I guess.

Now I just need somewhere good to read. "Hey house! You got a bed to read on around here?" I start looking for one and, sure enough, down a side passage I find a fully equipped bedroom with a massive bed. Not looking a gift horse in the mouth, I hop in it and start reading away.

A few hours later, I realize a few hours have passed. This book is actually really tricky; I'm still in the first chapter. It's like 60 pages, so it should be more than one chapter, but I can normally knock this out in that time. This book keeps making me re-read earlier parts just to make sense of new parts; you have to read it in circles for it to make any kind of sense.

It's just about time to consider maybe sleeping. Should I use this bed or try and find my way home? Eh, fifty-fifty odds say I'm just dreaming right now anyway, with all this craziness, so why not just sleep here? Besides, that bed is pretty nice and nobody's expecting me anywhere until at least Monday. So, I'll sleep in here.

A while later, I wake up. Checking my phone, I see it's 9:00 in the morning; haven't seen this hour in a while. Well, I'm still here, so no time like the present. Let take a look around this house. Grabbing my book on the way out, I step into the hallway.

Wait, I need to leave and get my meds. Backtracking, I quickly find the door I entered from. Slipping out, I find myself back outside the old house. I guess that makes sense in a "crazy magic house" sort of way. I just hope I can get back in. Letting myself back out of the gate, I walk home and get my meds along with a change of clothes; for all I know, the House has those hiding somewhere, but let's not bank on it.

Anything else I need? Let's take my big bag; could use it for carrying books and stuff. In fact, I'll put everything in there right now. Magic book, drugs, clothes, keys... my phone's charger, can't forget that. I didn't check if the House has anywhere to plug in, actually. Here's hoping it has that and WiFi.

Once more unto the breach. I let myself back into the old gate and slip back into the door. It still works; I'm back in the entry chamber. Stepping out in the main hall, I see some girl sitting in a chair wearing cliché bright purple robes- she seems to be half reading, half blowing her long fiery red hair out of her eyes.

"Hey." I call out to grab her attention. "Do you know what's up with this place?"

"Does anyone really? I mean, I know-"

"Let's not get too deep into it. I just got here yesterday and I need to know what I should be doing here."

"Do you know what you want to do?"

"No."

"Then do anything." She's full of whimsy, it seems. "Hopefully, a path will find you. Picking up a book or two-"

"Already did that."

"Getting ahead of me. You seem to have a good idea what you're doing already. Just read and look around. The books will teach you many new things. Paying attention to the house around you can reveal insights, as well. If you need food or something, just go looking for it; the House provides such things as they are needed."

"And where do I find a power outlet?"

"Your room should have a few. There are others, but start there."

"My room? I have a room?"

"You slept here last night, didn't you?"

"Yeah." I guess she noticed that.

"That's your room now. You can keep it."

"Oh. Good."

"Well, welcome to the House. I'm usually wandering around or reading here in the entryway to greet new keyholders. I'm Erica Handler, by the way."

"Alexis Mon- er, Stormbraid; Alexis Stormbraid. Keyholder?"

"Just a term a few of us use to refer to those the House chose to let in. We say we have the key to get in."

"The House chooses?"

"Yeah, it picks people to give a key to; it seems to pick people it thinks it can help."

"Should I be off-" I stop and laugh. "Nah, I'm a mess; I'm sure it can help me somehow."

"That's a good outlook, I suppose. Anyway, if you need anything else, do get in touch. Also, if you see a talking cat named Simon, tell him I'm looking for him; he keeps trying to avoid me."

"I will. Thanks. Bye."

"Farewell for now."

And she goes back to her book. Well, she seems... nice if odd. I could use some breakfast. Has that dining room restocked... No, it has vanished entirely instead. Great. There's got to be food around here somewhere; Erica just said the House would handle this. I've just got to find it... The library is gone too...

This house definitely moves things around. My room's door is still here. Behind it... a dining room with breakfast. Well, that is what I was looking for. I'll take it for now.

One filling breakfast later, I try and head back to my room. Not sure how, given that it's supposed to be behind the door I just left, but here we go. A few minutes wandering later, I stumble upon another door. Opening it, I find a bedroom... with a full glass of water on the table. Is this my room again? I didn't leave the water, but this crazy house could have put that there. I guess it would be my room; it's what I was looking for and that does seem to be this house's method of operation.

As predicted, there are outlets in here. Plugging in my phone, I start reading my magic book some more. A few minutes later, my phone rings... I guess I still have service here. It's Alice again; she's likely trying to check on me. Better answer or she'll come over and I'll have to rush home.

"Good morning, Alice."

"Alexis! You sound cheerful today."

"Heh, guess I woke up on the right side of the bed this morning."

"That's good." She sounds relieved. "Still home alone?"

"Yeah. Just me and a good book. All I really need in this world."

"Well, that's great. You sounded really bad yesterday, so I was worried."

"Well, is there anything else? Cuz if not, I'm just getting to the really good part here." She knows how I like my books, so she should take that.

"I'll leave you to it then. Bye."

"Bye."

I spend the next few hours trying to crack my way into this book. It is starting to get a bit easier to advance. It seems to trying to teach me to magically enhance my mind; this part is all about memory. I guess a photographic memory would be helpful in learning magic; it would help me remember the proper name for that ability, for starters.

As I look up, a large grey cat walks in the room. He looks a bit cute, but he's also looking around with intention. I kneel down to pet him, but he pulls back away and just stares at me.

"Hello, little guy. Are you Simon?"

"Yeah. What's it to ya?" Alright, so cats can actually talk here; she wasn't joking.

"Erica's-"

He cuts me off. "Looking for me. I know. She still owes me an apology, so no."

"What for?"

"Let's not air that here; it's complicated. So, I see you's a newbie around here."

"I suppose. You can talk?"

"Yeah. I'm a familiar; we all can. You'll get one eventually; don't worry about it until then. So, you got any other questions?"

"Not right now; Erica handled everything."

"Oh, guess I'm not needed here then. See ya 'round."

And he leaves the room, the door closing itself behind him. So either the cat can do magic or the House closed it; either way, I'll take it... Wait, there is a clock on the wall; its time matches my phone, which is locked to my time zone. I guess the House is either in my time zone or it knew what time it is for me and set my clock to match. Neat.

Anyway, back to the book until lunch time. It's starting to talk about building a mental world - what it is calling a Mind Palace. I guess you can store ideas in it to make them easier to understand and remember; I think that's the idea anyway. It's a bit strange. I'm not sure why you would need that, but I'll see where this goes.

By the time the evening runs around, I've actually had to straight up restart this chapter several times; the circles this book expects me to read in keep looping and re-looping. But it's all interesting, so... I'll follow this spiral all the way to the bottom.

Slipping back out of the House and back home, I find that someone delivered another package while I was away. It's not mine, so it must be my dad's; I just stick it in the middle of the living room and leave it. Slipping into bed for the night, I just hope he got eaten by a shark or something and doesn't come home. Sweet dreams indeed.

CHAPTER 3

In the morning, I'm awoken by a polite knocking on the door. Odd. Walking over, I see that Alice is at the door in her signature sky blue jacket. Even odder.

"Hello? It's not Thursday yet, is it?"

"No, it's not. I'm here to speak with your dad."

"Unless he snuck in last night- which really isn't like him- he's not here."

"Do you mind if I take a look around?" Her eyes are sweeping around the room.

"Go ahead."

As she wanders around, I'm not sure what she's thinking. Does she think he'll be hiding under the sofa or something? He wouldn't even fit under the sofa.

"Is something going on?

Alice sighs. "I'm worried. He should be here; he's not really allowed to leave you alone here."

"Frankly, I don't mind. I can handle myself."

"That's not a good thing either... bad phrasing. You shouldn't have to; the fact that you can is a good thing, but that shouldn't be a skill you need here. Are you sure he's not here?"

"Pretty sure. I don't see him anywhere and he's not exactly sneaky."

"Fair." She pauses in her search, seemingly surprised. "Why is there a wad of cash hiding in the bottom of the couch?"

"Good question. That one's not mine."

"That one? Is there more?"

"No..."

"So, yes then. You and your dad are both hiding things around the house. That's not good."

"Can we not talk about this?"

"Talking about this is my job. This is a sign of something unhealthy. So why are you hiding things?"

Now it's my turn to sigh. "To stop him from taking them, usually. He doesn't have much respect for my stuff."

"And why is he hiding stuff?"

"Presumably to stop me from taking them. If he's going to take my stuff, I need to take it back."

"Well... I'll have a word with him about that when he gets here... Where is all the food? This kitchen is empty."

"Is that so?"

"You've got that hidden somewhere too, don't you?"

"... Yeah. I paid for it myself; I'll put it where I want it."

"We'll deal with that later too. Did you take your pills yet today?"

"You woke me up not ten minutes ago. No. As I've told you before, I have an alarm set."

"Good. Look, when he gets here, call me right away. I really need to talk to him."

"I'll make sure to do that."

"Alright. Don't be afraid to call if you need to either."

"I know."

"Enjoy your day, Alexis."

"I'll try. Bye."

And she's gone. She wasn't supposed to be here today. She's not really supposed to come here at all; pretty sure it's outside her job description. But she does anyway. I know she's just trying to help me, but it gets annoying.

Well, he hasn't come home yet. That's nice. Let's just quickly get online and knock out my school work for the day while things are still quiet and peaceful.

A few hours later, I finish up my school work and take my meds. It's just about noon now and it's time to head over to the bookstore for work. Hopefully, things are kind of slow today... actually no, I think I can handle some speed today.

The bosses at this little bookstore are nice people; they don't really care what I do while nothing is happening as long as I don't cause any problems, so I'm always reading a book between customers here. Today, my book of choice is my magic book... Basic Uses of Inner Power, according to the title page.

Today is actually really slow, so I can get further into my book. As it advances deeper into chapter 1- which is really misnamed; it needs to be broken into several chapters- it starts trying to impart more mental enhancements. At this stage, it is trying to provide magic that helps me think faster. Sounds useful.

By the end of the shift, I've broken what I think is the midpoint of this chapter's looping. I think. The boss counts the cash into my hand and I walk back home.

As I walk up to the house, I see that the car isn't here yet. He hasn't gotten home yet. Now I'm worried; I don't like him, but he is responsible for paying for the big things. I think I have to call Alice about this. I don't really want to, but it's the responsible thing to do.

"Hey."

"Alexis! Is your dad there?"

"No, but he should be by now. That's why I'm calling."

"Oh." She pauses for a moment; to think, I'd assume. "I'll be right over."

"... Alright."

I knew she'd come over for that, but I still don't want her here. While she's on her way, I guess I'll start making something for dinner; if she's coming, I can't go over to the House for dinner... I think I forgot to eat breakfast. Again. Better not let her know that; she give me that judgment look of hers.

I'll make some extra dinner for her; she is taking time out of her day for this... Oh. She sent me a text. "I'll handle dinner." Well, scrap my plans. If she's got it, I'll let her get it. Surprising that she would bother though; that's way outside of her job description. I guess she's feeling really nice today.

I just curl up in the front room with my book until I hear a knocking on the door. Walking over, I open the door to let her in.

"Hey. I brought some fast food."

"Good thing you texted me when you did. I was about to start cooking some... something when you did."

"Glad I cut you off then. So, he's not here yet?"

"No, he isn't."

"Have you heard from him at all?"

"If I had, I'd have said something."

"Alright. If he's not here, I really can't let you stay-"

She wants to take me away from here; of course she does. "I don't want to-"

"I'm not really asking. I've got to do something here. Some-

23

thing has clearly happened and we need to find out what."

"Yeah, and I can do that from here."

"It's not safe for you to be home alone."

"This is way, way outside your job description. Are you supposed to-"

"My job right now is to make sure you are okay. And this..." She gestures around the room. "...is not okay."

"Everything is fine here. I am just fine staying here."

"You may think that, but you're not. You really weren't fine for the weekend either, but your dad said where he was going, so..."

"Fine. Where are we going?"

"I was just going to take you to my house until they find your dad, unless you've got a relative in the city you haven't told me about yet."

"If I've got them, I don't know them. I guess we can go to your house."

"You need help gathering things?"

"My bag actually already has all the important stuff in it. A change of clothes are all I really need to get. I'll go get that now."

So, I'm going to stay at her house for now, apparently. I guess that's fine. She's nice enough. It will be just fine. As long as I get to work- and she knows I need to do that... actually, I don't think she knows where exactly I work. I normally walk to work, so I might need a ride.

"Hey, where do you live?"

"Over near my office. Why?"

"The bookstore. I just needed to know if I need to arrange a ride there tomorrow or if I can walk like normal. Going to have to arrange a ride from there."

"Oh, I can get you there. Not a problem." That's a relief; one problem solved.

"Good. I'm ready by the way. I grabbed a couple outfits, just in case."

"Alright. Let's eat before we go."

"Fair. I am quite hungry..." Looking around, I realize I'm missing something. "Did you see where I sat my book?"

"Table over there."

"Oh, thanks." I slip it back into my bag.

"Odd looking book. Where'd you get it?"

"Bookstore. Thought it looked neat. Bought it."

"What's it about?"

"It's about... magic, actually. Like fake real magic, not real fake magic."

"Huh?"

"It claims to be about real magic, like wizards and spells and stuff, but it doesn't work- for obvious reasons."

"Oh. Neat." Good, she bought it. I don't know if I'm supposed to tell people about the House... or if anyone would believe me. Alice would likely think I'm insane. I'm still not sure I'm not.

The trip to her house is quick and easy, as I'd expect. Her office isn't that far away from my house. Normally, I take the bus when I come over to this end of town, but here we are.

"And we're here. Come on in; I'll show you around."

"K."

"Enthusiastic as always. Look over here. This is the guest bedroom; you're welcome to use it as long as you need it. At this hour, I imagine you are about to curl up in there until morning."

"You know me so well." And so I do so.

Tucking up into this bed, I guess I should try practicing something here. The current page is as good as any, talking about a Mind Palace. The book says I should close my eyes and focus, trying to go into the world within my own mind. As I focus, I feel myself drifting away.

I find myself in a blank white room. The room is filled with a light glow. This is kind of trippy. Alright, what was I supposed to do next? I think I'm supposed to be able to change this place with my mind; it is in my mind, after all. Let's try something simple. I imagine a table popping into existence in front of me... and a plain white table appears in front of me. That worked.

A few hours later, I finish rearranging this place to suit my will... the flying hot tub may have been a bit excessive, but the bookshelf with memory books on it should prove helpful. Having my life story and all the stuff I remember from school sitting here in book form should be very helpful.

Of course, is this even really magic? I remember seeing non-magical characters on TV do this kind of thing. I think. The book claims that this stuff is magic, but so far it seems to be just stuff that I'm pretty sure doesn't need magic.

When I open my eyes, the first thing I see is a clock on the wall... It says it's 9:30... I went in around 9:00. I was only in there about half an hour? Strange. I guess time moves different inside your own head. Well, let's go back to reading then.

As the book- er, chapter- proceeds, it drifts into a new subject: controlling your own mind. Taking control over your emotions and thoughts. Alice has been trying to teach me that trick for years, so I doubt the book will be overly effective in teaching this one. But we can try.

The next thing I know, I'm waking up and it's 10 in the morning. My book is laying under me, still open onto the page that

I was reading. It's trying to talk about... memory again, I think. Pretty sure I looped back to get to this point; the page looks like I've read it a few times before.

Slipping out into what I'm pretty sure is the living room, I see that Alice left some donuts on the table. That's nice of her. I sit down and open back up my book. I've got a few hours to spare before... I guess my schoolwork. The book is getting easier to continue as I read on, which is good. I'm starting to punch through the circles. I'm also pretty sure I'm memorizing many of these pages, so I don't even need to flip back; I just re-read them in my head. I guess the memory stuff is working.

An hour later, I am disturbed by my phone ringing. A glance reveals that it is my dad calling. One deep breath later, I answer.

"Hello."

"Who is this?" It's not my dad's voice.

"I could ask you the same. You called me, after all."

"Yeah. I found this phone lying on the floor in a bar. I just called the first number in the list. Are you Alex?"

"Alexis." Of course he didn't change it. "That's my dad's phone you're calling from. Where are you?"

"The Blue Ox."

"Great. Can you just give it to the cashier at the bookstore next door? Tell them I said to stick it in the register. I work there and I'll get it later."

"Alright. That works."

"Thank you. I need to call someone else now."

"Bye."

Alright. Alice needs to know about this. I call her, but it rings through to voicemail. She must be busy. I'll just wait and go back to reading. Another hour- by the end of which I think I'm closing in on the end of this chapter- later, Alice calls back.

"Alexis! Sorry I didn't-"

"It's fine. You have other patients who need you. Anyway, my dad's phone turned up in a bar. It's actually the one next to the bookstore. I had them leave it there; I can pick it up while I'm there."

"His phone? I assume he left it there then. Why didn't you try calling him before?"

"I almost never call him. If he went somewhere, he wouldn't answer anyway."

"I grow more concerned with every new detail, Alexis." She's said that a million times.

"I know. I just thought you needed to know all of this."

"I'm glad you called. I'll... deal with it later."

"Alright."

"I've got to-"

I jump in. "Get to your next client?"

"Yeah."

"I'll leave you to it then. Bye."

Well, this is... news. Can't say if it's good news or bad news yet, but it is news nevertheless. That bar is pretty far from the beach he claims to have been at; the closest beach, which is where I thought he was going, is... quick Google search... a 90 minute drive away. The closest bar to that beach is... on that beach. If he wanted a few drinks- which he very much would- he would go there. Him going to the Blue Ox means either he went way out of his way or he lied and never went to the beach at all.

He lied. That's the only answer that makes sense. But why would he do that? The only reason I can think of is... it meant I wouldn't start looking for him until Monday at the earliest. It gave him a two day head start.

No, that's not the only option. He could have been robbed at the beach and the person who stole his phone left it at the bar for being a worthless crap phone. But if that were the case, then he would have turned up by now. So, him lying is still more likely.

So, he lied to get a head start while he ran away... no, that's jumping to conclusions... he could have gone to the beach and then been attacked by a crazed gunman... no, I'd have heard about such an attack... right? Time for another Google search... nope, no such attack in the news. Running away seems the most likely answer.

Huh. I thought I would be the one to wind up running away from him. He's a horrible pile of shit. He's never there and when he is, he's an asshole.

Anyway, it's not like I can do anything about him vanishing. I'm stuck sitting here; even if I did go to walk somewhere, I don't know where anything is on this end of town except Alice's office and a bus stop. So, it's not worth worrying about right now. Just read my book and do my school work. That's all I can do.

CHAPTER 4

My phone seems to be loading slower than normal today. It's kind of annoying; it's going to make my schoolwork take hours. I'd best start early or I'll never finish it...

What is going on around here? I spend what was clearly 2 hours doing school work, which normally takes an hour except for my stupid phone, but only half an hour passed. All the clocks agree except for my mind... Did the book do this?

Wait. What if my phone's not slow... but I'm fast? Flipping back through the magic book, I remember that it did talk about speeding up the speed at which you think and see to allow you to do stuff faster. Maybe, I did get that working... now how do I turn it off? I think I just... think about it, I guess; it is all in my head, after all. A few minutes of staring at a clock later, I've figured out how to control the rate that time passes by.

Now I've got two "spells" to hand: Time Control and Mind Palace. I wonder what else I learned without realizing it. Let's test this.

The book started with stuff about memory, so we'll start there. Flipping through chapter one of the book, I try and memorize each page as I look at it. Alright, now let's see if I can read it in my Palace. Close my eyes and slip inside my inner world. My room is exactly as I left it. Perhaps I should remove the hot tub... nah. Let's see if I can recreate the book... Here it is!

Wait. I can't tell if it's correct or not. Of course it looks like I remember it, but my memory is what I'm testing! New plan, before I try and rely on that version of the book.

Let's just see if I can find a memory testing game online. Ah, here we go; a Simon knock off will get the job done... Half an hour later, I have to stop; the game was ready to keep going, but I think

100 in a row proves the point. So, I did get the perfect memory while I wasn't looking. That's nice... I know what I can do.

I'll memorize every page of the textbook, so I can just read it in my head later. Time passes much slower in there... what if I try to think faster while I'm in there? One thing at a time. Quickly flipping through the book, I take a snapshot of each page to read later. It seems memorizing things this way doesn't impart the knowledge to me, it just lets me recall it later. Still have to put in the effort.

Alright, so that just leaves emotion and thought control and I've finished chapter 1. Since there's no one watching, I'll just skip that for now; it's not like it's on the exam, after all. I may need some time reviewing before I can even begin to use that one.

Starting into Chapter 2, I find it has a complete change of subject matter. Where Chapter 1 covered enhancing one's mind with magical skills, Chapter 2 seems to cover enhancing one's body. Becoming faster and stronger is where it begins. Mind over matter seems to be the word of the day. This seems even less magical than the last chapter... Then again, the last chapter did teach me all of that in, what, four days? Got the book Saturday, it's Tuesday now, that's four days. Good book. Very effective... Such read. Much book.

I may have been reading it too much. I'm pretty sure I've spent at least 50 hours reading it by now. Oh well, let's add some more hours to that tally. I've still got a couple before work strikes.

Pressing on into the second chapter, the first thing it is trying to do is add Haste to my growing list of spells. That sounds very useful, given that I can think so fast now; movement to match would be amazing. However, it also seems that I'm now at the bottom of a new pit of circles; that's less than ideal.

My reading is interrupted by Alice stopping by to take me to work. When I walk in the door, the morning cashier hands me my dad's phone and leaves. Slipping that into my pocket, I take up my seat behind the register and resume my reading until the first customer shows up.

Turns out my first customer for the day is Guy. He walks up to the register with some books in hand. I sit my book down and start totaling up his books.

"Isn't this backward? Don't you come to my counter?"

"First time for everything, I suppose."

"Well, it's nice to... wait, is that what I think it is?" Strange question to ask.

"Huh? This is a book. I'm sure you're familiar with them. If not, this store has a lot of them for sale."

"Heh. But really, is that Basic Uses?" Oh. Wait, what?

"I don't know what you're talking about." Let's play dumb; see where that gets us.

"You've been to the House. When?"

I sigh; he's got me. "Found it Saturday."

"Welcome to the club, then. It's a great place."

"I actually haven't been since Sunday, but that's just because stuff is happening."

"Well, I'll leave you to it then. So, what's the damage?"

I tell him his total and collect his cash. He leaves with a cheerful wave. Once he's gone, I slow the world down as much as I can to think... I guess it's really me speeding up, but details. He knows about the House. Guy's a keyholder. Well, that's something. I'll bear that in- wait, can he help teach- no, I'm sure he could, but I'm not going to ask him.

The rest of the shift passes without event, just reading my book and taking people's money when they want books. A couple people asked what I was reading; I just told them it was a boring book for school. They stopped caring after that. Eventually, the shift ends and Alice picks me up. Driving back, she starts up a conversation.

"Was the phone there?"

"Yeah, I got it right here." I hold up the phone.

"Good. I'll take a look at it when we get there."

"Alright."

When we reach her house, I hand off my dad's phone and sit in a chair with my book. As the book moves onward, the magical speak gets denser and more obvious. "Using the innate power of the mind, developed in the previous chapter, in order to take control over the body and use it to advance towards completing that which you will to be done." That's... wording. But does it work? Probably, given where I found it.

"He's still got your name-"

"Wrong in his contacts list. I know."

"Okay then. He doesn't have many other people in here. He's got you, me, his boss and a pizza place. Let's see if his boss knows anything."

She steps out of the room, but I can still hear her.

"No, I'm just using his phone. Have you seen him?"

"Not since Thursday? He was supposed to be there yesterday, right?"

"Look, if you hear from him, just call me." She gives them her phone number.

"I'll let you get back to work."

She steps back into the room.

"Well, they haven't heard from him."

"I know; hasn't been in since Thursday. I could still hear you over there."

"Well, that makes that easier. I've got to go make another call."

And she steps away to go somewhere I can't hear her. She's likely calling the police at this point to tell them that he's gone missing. As much as I'd rather she not, she does have to. I think she is actually legally required to do that. I think. I really can't do anything about that. So, I'll just have to not worry about it. Alice has gotten me very good at doing that.

This chapter's loops are different. It seems to be a series of smaller loops rather than the giant sweeping loops of the first chapter. At least, so far. There may be big loops I haven't seen yet. But this chapter seems easier than the last, so that's nice.

It feels like she's gone for about two hours. Of course, it was less than that; my speed was shifted up to read faster. Checking my phone reveals that it's only really been forty-five minutes when she returns.

"Okay. Unless something happens, I'm done for the day."

"Alright."

"Have you eaten?"

"A bit. I've got stuff in my bag."

"Do you need me to-"

"I'm fine. I've got more stuff in my bag if I get hungry." I say, holding up a bag of chips.

"Very well. What woo is your book on now?"

"Making yourself stronger and faster with positive thinking."

She laughs. "Sounds useful. If I've been doing my job, you should have plenty of that to go around."

"The book tried to help with that earlier, too. It has a section about controlling one's own thoughts and emotions."

"You need to learn that one. It would do good things for you."

"Ha, ha, ha."

"So, I'm going to let you keep reading your book. I've got my own to read... wait, did you do your homework?"

"Yes."

"Alright, I'll let you just read then."

Good. That's the way I prefer things to be. As I continue to read, I wish I could go back to the House. I could see if the House has anything useful for me. Perhaps someone who could teach me how to use the emotion control ability or Haste. I think it could find someone who can help me. But how can I get there?

It's too far to walk there. Alice would notice if I left and I still don't know if I'm allowed to tell her about the House... or able for that matter. She probably wouldn't believe me anyway. I'm pretty sure that I can't show her the place; would it let her in? I don't think it would.

I guess I can't get there right now. Shame, it could have been very useful. But I'm here and it's there. That settles that, then.

Time passes with little happening until Wednesday after work, when a cop shows up at Alice's house. I'd guess he's here about me... yeah, he is. He takes me off to a side room to talk; odd, I'd expect he'd want to go to the station for this. Eh, what do I know?

He asks me an array of questions about my dad: where could he have gone (no idea), who are his friends (no idea), why would he have left (he's an asshole), any useful information (no). Bit of a wasted trip on the cop's part.

After talking to me, he has a brief talk with Alice as well. If I had to guess, it's about whether me staying here is a good idea. If I'm safe here, if she minds, if she knows anyone else who should be watching me.

After he leaves, Alice just resumes writing whatever she was writing before he showed up. I guess the cop just left everything as it is. Fine by me; not really fond of cops, myself. If they stay out of my way, all will be well.

I need to test myself. These abilities don't seem make themselves apparent unless I test for them. To test my speed, I guess I need to go running down the block.

"I'm going to go for a walk. Get some fresh air. I'll be back later."

She calls over towards the door. "Okay."

I put on my jacket and go running down the street. Alright, so to make this thing work, I'm supposed to slow the world down by speeding my mind up; if it's working and I'm in the right frame of mind, my own movements will feel perfectly normal, because I'm moving as fast as I'm thinking. I just start running down the street; everything looks normal at first, but looking around the world is being a bit slow. It might be working. I think it is.

I could just go to the House from here. I've got my bus pass; I can just hop on a bus. Alice would be concerned, but I could still do it. The bus stop is right here... a 10 minute walk from where I started. I was only walking for... 5 minutes or so? Yeah, I got Haste working. I'm getting on the bus; hopefully the House can find me a teacher.

The bus drops me off down the street from the House. Walking over to the House, I check my phone to note the time. I don't want to be gone too long or Alice will get concerned. Slipping into the House, I start wandering around in the hopes of finding a teacher. I walk into a long hallway with a guy standing near me at one end. Suddenly, someone I can barely see at the other end of the hall shoots a bolt of lightning at the guy next to me; the guy next to me smacks the bolt into the wall. As he does, he notices that I am there.

"Stop! Safety issue." He shouts down the hallway at the guy over there, who sits down in a chair. "This is a rather dangerous room today. What brings you?"

"I was actually looking for a teacher of some kind. I wasn't looking for... whatever this is."

"This is a lesson on lightning bolts. You've found a teacher. I might be able help you, depending what you need and what kind of cash you've got."

"I actually need help with..." I pull out my book. As I'm flipping to the section on Emotion Control, he cuts me off.

"If it's something in there, I can likely help you with it in an hour or so."

"It's this." I show him the section.

"Oh, basic Emotion Control. Yeah, easy. Stop by here tomorrow around 9:00 PM. I'll be in the lobby. 20 bucks." That's a great deal.

"Deal. I'll see you then... You mean 9 in this time zone, right?"

"Oh, yeah. I always forget that kind of thing. I live in this time zone."

"Alright. I'll leave you to your... lightning, I guess."

As I walk away, I use my phone to check what time zone the House is in. It turns out the House is one hour behind of me, so I need to be here 10:00 my time. That also tells me the House did set the clock in my room to match my time zone.

Well, I found what I was looking for quickly. I should be able to get back to Alice's house before she notices that anything happened. As far as she needs to know, I just took a long walk.

I hop onto another bus to head back up to her end of town. Luckily for tomorrow, the buses run until midnight, so I should be able to take the bus there and back for my lessons; actually, I think they run a bit later than that, so I've got some leeway.

As I walk back up to Alice's house, I realize that I need to knock on the door because I don't have a key. I do so and Alice opens the door.

"Welcome back... I need to get you a key to get in here."

"Might be useful." Please do, I need to sneak out tomorrow night.

"Here, I should have a spare around here somewhere." After a brief look around, she grabs a key off a shelf and hands it to me.

"Thanks."

"Dinner's done, if you're hungry."

Sounds good. "Great. I'll have to grab some."

Grabbing some food, I tuck off into the room I'm using to eat and read. I've nothing else to do until... my appointment at Alice's office tomorrow, I guess. I also have schoolwork, but I don't think I need to rush that; I can knock that out very quickly now.

CHAPTER 5

By the time I have to go to Alice's office on Thursday, I'm buried in the circles of learning how to invoke super strength effectively by willing your muscles to work harder, which also doesn't sound like magic, but what do I know anymore?

I take up my familiar chair in the familiar office as Alice begins to talk.

"I'd say 'Glad you could make it here today.', but I did drive you here."

"Yeah, that wouldn't make much sense."

"I mean, I am glad you're here, but..." She laughs. "Let's get started."

Ninety minutes later, my appointment comes to an end. No new groundbreaking revelations today; just more of the same. Talking about who I am and who I really am. This visit had a nice side topic of exactly what kind of shitpile my dad is, but that's not really a new subject either.

She always seems to know what I'm thinking. I imagine it comes with the job, but it feels like her steel blue eyes can see right through me.

After all of that is done, I've got a spare hour to kill before work. Doing my schoolwork quickly only takes up half of that time, so I guess it's back to Basic Uses of Inner Power. I've got to get this power... I'll call it Bull's Strength... worked out.

At work, things are quite boring for most of the shift. But towards the very end of the shift, Guy walks up holding a book. It's an odd-looking book. Not really surprised; a lot of our books look odd. It does look slightly familiar though.

"Do you know where this place gets its books?" He seems

slightly worried.

"Not really sure. Why?"

"Because this is a copy of Guide to the Spirit World. It's from the House. It's not supposed to be here." Oh. That's a problem... I think.

"Oh. What do..."

"You don't need to do anything here. Other than charge me for it, I guess."

"I can do that. Question though: Is the House a secret? I kind of just assumed it was; that is how stories like this tend go, after all."

"Not really. There aren't really any rules at the House at all. You can tell people if you really want to."

"Why haven't I heard about it before then? You would think it would be all over the internet by now."

"Your guess is as good as mine. Stories about it seem to have a resistance to being spread. I've always guessed the House somehow quiets them down, but I've no idea how it would."

"Well then." That's... strange.

"Here's the cash. I've got to go return this to where it belongs. Have a good evening."

Eventually, everything winds down and Alice takes me back to her house. I just tuck off into the corner with some food until Alice goes to bed. One night of her going to bed early is one thing; three reveals a pattern. I guess it makes sense; I think she has clients at like six or seven in the morning.

Slipping out the front door, I make sure to lock it behind me; lock it from the outside to make sure I have the key. I dash down to the bus stop, arriving just as the bus pulls up; memorizing the schedule has its benefits. The bus drops me off down the street from my house once again and I quietly slip into the House.

I'm about thirty minutes early, so I just take a seat and wait. Twenty minutes later, teacher guy walks into the room; I should get his name.

"You're early, Alexis."

"I had to take a bus..." Wait a tick; hold the phone. "I never gave you my name."

"Telepath. Anyway, let's get started. Come on."

He leads me up a staircase and into a large circular room.

"Here we are. First order of business: my money."

"Oh yeah. Here." I hand him a $20 bill.

"Perfect. Now then, you needed help learning Emotion Control? Odd, usually that one's not much of a stopping point."

"My emotion control is so bad I take drugs for it."

"Ah. I see. Alright, take a seat, grab my hand and close your eyes."

I do so and suddenly find myself in a different room. The walls are made of red sandstone. A soft white light fills the entire room. The room is empty except for me and teacher guy.

"Where are we?"

"In my Mind Palace. If we're learning a mental ability, we may as well do it in a mind, so we can do it faster."

"You can do that?!"

"It's pretty tricky, but yeah, I can. So, let's begin."

"Before we do, something has been bothering me. I never got your name."

"You can call me Ed. Now, let's get down to business."

As it happens, there wasn't any secret to Emotion Control that I didn't see; you have to use your focus and will to take control of your own mind, allowing you to suppress emotions and pain to help maintain focus. It's just really hard for me and takes a lot of practice. Ed spends what feels like about 2 hours helping me get a handle on using this power; by the end of it, I feel like I've got this under control.

"Alright, I'd say you've got it." He says, bringing an end to the lesson.

"I think so."

"Well then. Let's get out of here. Close your eyes."

I do. A few moments later, I open them again to find myself back in the chair I started in.

"You're in luck. That only took half an hour. You've still got me for another half an hour, so you're getting a two-for-one deal. What are you up to in Basic Uses?"

"Super strength."

"Good spot to be. I can help with that. You've got super speed under control already, right?"

"Yeah, that's working."

"Good, it's actually required if you want to use super strength."

He then spends the next half hour teaching me how to use super strength. He's actually a really good teacher; by the time he's done, I've think I've got it working. I really got my money's worth on this guy.

His phone goes off. He just pulls it out and taps it, stopping the sound.

"And that's time."

"So it is. That was a crazy hour. Thanks for that."

"Pleasure doing business with you." And with that, he leaves the room and slips into another.

I slip back out of the House and over to my house; I've got twenty minutes to kill before the bus gets here to take me back. Might as well check the mail... it's empty. I guess Alice must have cleared it already.

As I enter the living room, the package in the middle of the room is gone. Okay, either Alice took it or my dad was here... and Alice doesn't have a key. His car's not here; he's not here now. He probably just dashed through for his package, but... Looking around, the box was discarded in the kitchen. The paper inside reveals that he bought... a sword? Doesn't seem like his kind of package.

I'm just taking a seat in the living room when I have an idea. Hopping up, I walk over and pick up the sofa; yep, Bull's Strength is go. Sitting the sofa back down, I sit on it for a few minutes.

Suddenly, I hear a knocking on the door. Since I'm not really supposed to be here, I ignore it. Then, a loud crack echoes forth from the door; they kicked it down. Need to slow the world down to think.

Stay calm; you just learned how to do this. If you lose your wits now, you could be... let's not go there; I need to stay calm. I can't go alone here; I need help. I guess Alice will have know I'm here. One quick text later, she knows I'm here and in danger; I just hope her phone wakes her up.

Okay, next: survey the threat. Run over there and peak around the corner. This guy is just now clearing the door; slow-mo for the win. He's got a handgun, which sucks for me. He also appears to be alone.

Suddenly, he starts moving much faster... He's moving at normal speed... in my slow-mo vision. Crap. He's got super speed too. New plan: hide in the House. I just have to get there. I rush over and grab the couch, throwing it at him. He clearly didn't expect me to be able to do that, since it hit him.

He pushes the couch aside a moment later and starts shooting at me. Woah. This looks trippy. I can see the bullets as they fly. Wait, I think he's slowed down more; did my super speed get better while I wasn't looking? Anyway, I can see the bullets and can move fast enough to not get hit by them. I can dodge the bullets. Cool.

Running towards the gunman, I roll under the bullets as he's shooting higher up. He's blocking the only exit, so I have to get past him. Or do I? I'm right next to him; I could try to take his gun. No, that's too risky; he could have more speed too. Just run.

Running over to the old house, I see there is someone else standing in front of the door. This guy has a knife; not as bad, but his friend is still behind me. Guns are loud; presumably someone will have called the cops by now... I'm in super speed. Even if the cops somehow show up in just 5 minutes, I'd have to survive 20 minutes at this speed. Alice is a 10 to 15 minute drive away, so almost an hour at this speed. No one can save me out here.

I have to get into the House and hope it can protect me until backup arrives. I have to engage the knife guy and go through him. As I charge at him, he moves to swing his knife; he seems to be moving super slow, so he doesn't have super speed. This should be easy.

I move under the knife and punch this guy in the face. The gunman has clearly made it outside, as he takes a shot in my direction; fortunately, he missed, but not by much. Slipping past knife guy, I open and slip in the door to the House, holding it closed behind me.

They aren't trying to open it. That door doesn't work for them. Okay, I'm safe for now. Next: if I've brought Alice in, I need to tell her what's going on. She's either asleep and will panic in the morning or her phone woke her up and she's driving over now. Either way, I need to call her now.

She answers instantly; clearly she was already up. "What's going on?"

"You aren't going to believe any of this, but I swear it's all true."

"Go on."

"Okay, so I've got... hold on, context: on Saturday I found a strange magical House- rather, I found a portal to it- and I snuck over to it tonight -- someone was helping me study magic -- yeah, that woo book I'm reading is actually real and from this House." I pause to breathe. "Anyway, I went over to my house to wait for the bus and then a guy with a gun kicked down the door. I managed to slip past him and escaped. I'm currently hiding in the House; the magical one, that is."

"You're right; normally, I wouldn't believe that. Tonight, on the other hand, I kinda do. I'm on my way over right now. Are you safe?"

"Yeah. I don't think they can get in here."

"They? Is there more than one?"

"Yeah. There's another guy with a knife right in front of the door I use to get here. Er, the portal is a door."

"Alright, are they still there?"

"I don't know. I can't see from here. The cops are likely on their way; the gunman fired several shots at me."

"Oh. Are you-"

"I'm fine. If I'd been hit, I'd have mentioned that sooner."

"So he's a bad shot. That's good I guess. I'll make sure the cops are coming. I'm going to hang up and call back when I get there."

"K."

And she hangs up. A couple minutes later, Simon walks into my exit room and walks over.

"You okay? You look a bit rattled."

"I just had a guy shooting at me with super speed."

"Oh... Well then... I'm going to go get Erica; that's serious. Hold on."

Simon runs out of the room in a hurry. A few minutes later, my phone rings; it's Alice.

Before I can say anything, she starts talking. "The cops were already on their way. One of your neighbors had called it in."

"Good... Wait, no. They could be in walking into great danger. I only survived because I've worked out how to move fast enough to dodge bullets... which the gunman can also do. He could curbs-tomp them."

"Oh. I don't think I can really tell them that. They wouldn't believe me if I tried. They know he's armed, so hopefully they are prepared to handle it."

"Hopefully."

"Ok, I'm parked down the street from your house. Where is this portal?"

"The old house next door. I think it only lets me use it."

A voice from the door suddenly reveals itself; it's Erica.

"Only Keyholders can use a Door."

Lowering my phone, I respond. "Okay... Wait, who can use it?"

"Only those the House itself allows in. We covered this." I knew that.

"Right, freaking out here. I'll be with you in just a minute." And I go back to my phone.

"Okay, so people can only come in if the House lets them. I figure those guys aren't on the list."

"Good. They are standing outside that house. I think they are waiting for you to come back out. Who's that on your end?"

"Erica. She's nice."

"Alright. I'm going to try and see what else is going on. I'll call you back."

And she hung up. Okay, Erica is here.

"Hello."

"You've got an Evil Wizard out there?"

"You could say that."

"No, that's a proper noun. Evil Wizard."

"Oh. I don't know then. I've got an evil wizard- two of them really- but I don't know if they are Evil Wizards. How do you know?"

"If they're a member of this group called the Evil Wizards. But you wouldn't know how to tell. Do you mind if I jump in and help?"

"They have-"

"Guns, I know. It's fine; I've fought them before."

"Have at it. I'll hide in the hall."

"Alright."

From the hall, I see Erica open the door and step through it, closing it behind her. She steps back in the room a minute later.

"There. Got them handled. You should be safe to go out there now. Left them bound up for the cops. Have a good... it was dark out there, so good night." And she leaves.

CHAPTER 6

I step out of the door and see Alice standing nearby. The two attackers are bound up in tight ropes and there are scorch marks on the ground.

"What happened?"

"Someone came out and-"

"That's Erica."

"Well, she came out and snapped her fingers, lighting the area on fire. Both of these idiots fell to the ground and she tied them up in the blink of an eye. Somehow, they aren't burnt."

"I guess that works. She just offered to deal with them for me and then did this."

A cop car pulls up. Alice walks over and talks to them. One of them takes me off to the side and asks me what happened.

I explain the best I can. "I was just waiting at home and this guy came in, kicking down the door and swinging a gun around. I managed to get past him and hide until you guys got here."

"How did they get tied up?"

"I don't know. Superheroes would be my best guess."

"Ha ha. Do you have any idea who they are?"

"No idea."

A few more pointless questions and a conversation with someone across the street later, he takes the dingbat attackers, grabs their gun and leaves. Alice directs me into her car and drives me back to her house. As she's driving, she starts asking me questions.

"So, why did you sneak out?"

"I had an appointment with a guy who was helping teach me some of this stuff." I hold up Basic Uses. She sighs.

"You could have just asked me. I could have driven you there or at least known you were going."

"Then I'd have had to explain the whole 'learning magic' thing, which I didn't want to do."

"...fair." She pauses for a moment, focusing on the road. "What'd you learn?"

"Focus and super strength."

"Okay then." She seems confused, but too tired to do anything about it.

We reach her house and both go to bed.

In the morning, I hop up and walk out, sitting down in the living room. Alice is already gone, so I'm alone again until work. Perfect. I'm on an early shift today, but I've got time to press deeper into this book.

Woah. The next section seems to be teaching a power they call Repletion. If I'm reading this right, it lets you slow down your body's need for things like food or sleep so you don't need them as much. That sounds very useful. As I start reading, I hear a knocking on the door. Looking out a window, I see that it's Guy. I open the door.

"What brings you?"

"I heard about the Evil Wizard attack yesterday. You okay?"

"I'm fine. Bit shaken I guess, but I can handle that now."

"Good."

"Why did they attack me?"

"Because you're allowed into the House. They're looking to kill such people and take any magical books they have."

"They aren't allowed in, then?"

"Yeah. Some were never chosen, while others were kicked out... Expelled, if you like."

"Oh. I thought you said there weren't any real rules."

"There aren't, really. But the House kicks people out if they... become evil, I suppose. The House seems to have morals."

"Oh... But if they get their hands on magical books..."

"They can use them anyway, that's correct. Some of us- like myself- are trying to find and stop them. Others can't be bothered to care; they just keep their heads down and defend themselves if need be." He stops for a moment as I sigh. "I'm not going to try and drag you into my crusade, don't worry."

"Do you know how they knew I was-"

"The blame for that likely lands on me. As I found out yesterday, one of them has been stalking me. Likely overheard me talking to you at the bookstore. He's been dealt with."

"Oh."

"I'm going to get going now. Stay on your guard."

"Okay... Wait. This is going to be an embarrassing question, but if this crap is happening now, I need to know: I've never actually learned your name."

He laughs. "You've seen my nametag how many times? I'm Oliver. Should probably give you my phone number too." He writes it down on the back of a random receipt and hands it to me. "Call me if any more of those punks shows up."

"Thank you."

Then he leaves and go back to my book. As I spiral around Repleation, I hear a strange noise deeper in the house. Hopping up, I find my way to a small study where I think the sound came from. Suddenly, a book falls from a small shelf and I jump back.

Picking up the book, I see it's a boring psych book and return it to the shelf. Watching the book, it appears an unseen force pulls the book forward and causing it to fall again. Catching the book, I put it back again.

"Who's doing that?" The book starts to move again, but I hold it in place. A different book starts to move, so I use my arms to block the whole row of books. "What's going on?" I feel a tapping on my shoulder, but there is no one there. I ramp down, slowing the world to a crawl to think. "Can you talk?" The strange force taps the back of my hand. Thinking quickly, I grab a piece of paper from the desk in here and a magnifying glass. Writing letters on the paper, I improvise a Ouija board. The magnifying glass jumps to the "H".

"H-E-L-L-O"

"What- who are you?"

"T-Y-S-O-N I A-M A S-P-I-R-I-T"

"Why are you here?"

"Y-O-U A-R-E K-E-Y-H-O-L-D-E-R R-I-G-H-T"

"Yeah."

"I A-M H-E-R-E T-O H-E-L-P"

"Do I need any?"

"E-V-I-L W-I-Z-A-R-D-S" The magnifying glass pauses for a moment. "T-H-A-T A-N-D Y-O-U-R D-A-D"

"What do you know about my dad?"

"A L-O-T U-S-E-D T-O B-E F-R-I-E-N-D-S"

"What? Are you, like, a ghost of someone he knew?"

"N-O" Another pause. "H-A-V-E Y-O-U N-O-T R-E-A-D A-B-O-U-T S-P-I-R-I-T-S Y-E-T"

"No. I'm still learning the basics. I've been at this less than a week... actually, I think it is a week by this point." I quickly add a question mark to the sheet; seems like it could be useful.

"O-H I M-A-Y H-A-V-E J-U-M-P-E-D T-H-E G-U-N"

"I guess?"

"S-P-I-R-I-T-S P-O-W-E-R E-L-E-M-E-N-T-A-L M-A-G-I-C I-T I-S W-H-E-R-E F-A-M-I-A-L-A-R-S C-O-M-E F-R-O-M"

"What does that- No. You're not saying...?"

"Y-O-U-R D-A-D W-A-S A K-E-Y-H-O-L-D-E-R I W-A-S H-I-S F-A-M-I-L-I-A-R"

"I notice the past tense."

"H-E W-A-S E-X-P-E-L-L-E-D I L-E-F-T H-I-M A-F-T-E-R T-H-A-T"

"Oh."

"Y-O-U W-E-R-E N-O-T B-O-R-N Y-E-T T-H-E-N" He pauses. "Y-O-U D-O N-O-T K-N-O-W H-O-W T-O B-I-N-D A F-A-M-I-L-I-A-R D-O Y-O-U-?"

"No. Like I said, still learning the basics." I hold up Basic Uses.

"O-K W-E N-E-E-D T-O G-O T-O T-H-E H-O-U-S-E G-E-T B-O-O-K-S"

"I can't right now. I'm can't leave until work. After work, I can take the bus there, but that's hours away."

"I C-A-N W-A-I-T I W-I-L-L J-U-S-T F-O-L-L-O-W Y-O-U"

"Alright. I'm going back to reading in the living room."

The magnifying glass slides back to where I grabbed it. I fold the paper up and take it with me. Settling back into the living room, I reopen Basic Uses and resume my spiraling into Repleation. Eventually, Alice shows up to take me to work. On the ride, I bring up an obvious point.

"You know, I can just take the bus. You don't have to drive me."

"Fair point except for the guys trying to kill you. What if more show up?"

"You'd rather be in the line of fire? I'll just have to get even better even faster so I can fight back if they come back."

She whistles. "I guess I've done my job well. The Alexis I first met... what, five years ago would have either panicked at the idea of someone trying to kill them or said 'thank god, someone wants to save me the trouble'. You charging into danger isn't good, either, but it's an improvement."

"And yet your solution is to put you in danger, as well."

"Surely they wouldn't attack if you had backup on hand?"

I cover my face with my hand. "Yeah, if I had backup that could make a difference in the fight. After that, they know what I can do and they'll send tougher stuff next time. You'd be Lois Lane versus... some supervillain. They'd just ignore you. I've just got to get better."

"I guess... I've got an idea. I'll tell you more when I pick you up."

Well, that's ominous. Sitting behind the register as always, I lay the spirit paper off to the side and put a quarter from my pocket on it.

"You still there?" I whisper as the quarter begins to move.

"Y-E-S S-H-E S-E-E-M-S N-I-C-E"

"Who? Alice? Yeah, she is."

"S-H-E T-H-E D-R-I-V-E-R-?"

"Yes."

"Y-E-A-H H-E-R S-H-E I-S N-I-C-E"

"Okay."

"I-S T-H-I-S W-H-E-R-E Y-O-U W-O-R-K-?"

"Yeah. I just run the register here."

"O-K" And the quarter slides off the paper.

The shift passes uneventfully until Alice returns. Tyson makes some snide comments about some customers, but nothing important. Climbing back into the car, I instantly resume my earlier conversation.

"So, what are you planning?"

"I think you might want to sign up for martial arts classes."

"Sounds like a waste of money."

"I think you-" She stops suddenly as a strange look passes over her face. "What was that?"

"What was what?"

"I felt something tap my shoulder."

"Oh right, that's Tyson. He's a spirit ghost thing who's following me right now. He actually needs us to go to the House."

"Like, now?"

"I think so? Tyson? ... Right, you can't talk." I dig around in my bag for something he can move, settling on a die. I sit it on my palm. "If you can move that, please do." The die flips sides. "Alright Tyson, if you can change the side, let's go evens for yes and odds for no. Alice?"

"Do you need to go right now?" The die flips to a 1. "Alright then... What are you exactly?"

I respond to her question, since he can't answer that. "Yes or no questions only right now; I can set up something better when we get there."

"Are you a ghost; like, are you a dead person?" The die rotates to a 3. "So you're just some kind of invisible spirit?" The die turns into a 2. "Alright. We'll talk more when we get home." The die tips over, revealing a 6.

As we walk into her house, I just unfold the paper, sit a quarter on it and sit down.

"Alice, meet Tyson. Tyson, meet Alice."

"H-E-L-L-O"

"Hello. So, why do you need to go to the House?"

"S-O S-H-E C-A-N L-E-A-R-N T-O B-I-N-D F-A-M-I-L-I-A-R-S"

"I assume you would become this familiar, then?"

"Y-E-S" I quickly jot the words 'Yes' and 'No' onto the paper; should save some time. "YES"

"Well, if you'd like, we can go do that after dinner. Sound good?"

"YES" And the quarter slides of the paper.

"Well, that's a plan... do you know how to bake-"

"Let me cut you off there. Unless it comes pre-prepared and frozen, the answer is no, I don't."

"Well, come on then. You need to learn."

An hour later, Alice and I have finished making and eating a pizza; came out pretty good, really.

"So, let's go."

"You know, we should stop by my house while we're over there. Gather up anything valuable so no one else can, since the door's broken."

"Yeah. I'll do that while you're in the House."

"Sounds like a plan."

We all get in the car... I assume Tyson got in the car; I can't see him, so it's just a guess... and start driving down the road. I fish out the die again.

"Tyson, you with us?" The die flips to a 2. "Good."

"Hey, Tyson. Do you think getting her into self-defense classes is a good idea?" The die flips to a 4.

"Traitor." I pocket the die.

"So why is he following you?"

"Oh, right. I didn't tell you yet. According to Tyson, my dad has been to the House before. He-"

"That's kind of a big deal."

"Yeah. Tyson was his familiar before. When my dad got kicked out of the House- oh yeah, that happened- Tyson abandoned him."

"How did he get kicked out?"

"No idea. Tyson didn't tell me. According to Guy- his name's Oliver, by the way; I actually asked him today- the House kicks people out if they become evil."

"So, your dad is evil?"

I briefly chuckle. "No news there."

"Ha, ha, ha. I'll ask Tyson later."

"You know, you're taking all this magic crap far better than I expected."

"It's happening and I can't do anything about it, so I'm just rolling forward with it. No sense worrying about problems you can't solve." Right. She's told me that a dozen times; it's practically her catchphrase.

"Okay then."

We reach my house and hop out. I walk over to my Door and enter the House. I just wander off, looking for the library... or a library, I guess; this place could have more than one. A few minutes of searching later, I find it and start looking around... for what?

"Okay, Tyson. I don't know what book I need. Can you knock it off the shelf for me?" A few minutes elapse- I assume he's looking for the book- before a book falls off a shelf nearby. "Thank you."

I grab the book and check the title: Binding and Channeling.

Sounds like what I need. Welp, I'm done here. I backtrack out of the House and return to my house. Alice has gathered a bunch of stuff in the center of the living room.

"I'm back."

Alice pops out of the kitchen. "Got a new book?"

"Yep. What have you turned up so far?"

"$1 thousand dollars cash, some tech stuff and a handgun." Alice goes back into the kitchen, but keeps talking. "I've already called someone to deal with the gun."

"Huh. Didn't know he had that."

"Well, I'm pretty sure he's not supposed to. He doesn't seem the type to have the license for this."

I sigh. "I wish you were wrong about that."

"So do I... Oh! I found a small safe hiding behind the wall. Let's see if I can-"

"12-32-22. He usually keeps money in there."

"Yeah. He's got another five hundred bucks in here... there's a secret panel in the bottom."

"What?" I go running into the kitchen. "I didn't know about that. What's in it?"

"A book. It looks like the one you've been reading actually."

"Let me look... Yeah, that's Basic Uses of Inner Power. As if we needed proof at this point. I'll take hold of that one; I think it needs to go back to the House later. First, I'm going to go read my new book."

Slipping back into the living room, I start reading Spirits and Binding... and instantly hit a wall of pure nonsense. I set up the spirit board.

"What do I need to know to make sense of this?"

"S-O-U-L S-I-G-H-T"

"The hell is that?!"

"F-I-R-S-T S-E-C-T-I-O-N O-F C-H-A-P-T-E-R T-H-R-E-E"

"I'm still in the middle of chapter two. I'm learning Repleation right now."

"O-H" He pauses for a few seconds. "Y-O-U M-I-G-H-T W-A-N-T T-O F-I-N-D H-E-L-P T-H-E-N"

Sigh. Let's see if Oliver can help. I do have his number after all.

"Hey. What's up?"

"I need your help in doing things out of order."

"Found a spirit too soon?"

"Yeah. How did you-"

"Happens sometimes. I've had to do this before. Where are you?"

"My house." I give him the address.

"On my way."

Well, that was easy. I guess this isn't a rare problem. As I'm waiting for him to get here, I resume my attempts to understand Repleation. Ten minutes later, I hear a knocking on the door... rather, the wall next to the door. I walk over and let Oliver in.

"Okay, let's get started. Do we need to visit the House or do you already have Binding and Channeling?"

"Got it right here."

"Perfect... Now we need to go to the animal shelter."

"What?!"

"Spirits are bound into an animal to create a familiar. Like Rose here." A small white mouse sticks its head out of his pocket. The mouse waves at me.

"Oh. I'd have to-"

Alice shouts down the stairs. "Just go! I'll meet you back at my house."

Oliver responds. "Well, that settles that. What's the spirit's name?"

"Tyson."

"Alright. Tyson, make sure to keep up."

CHAPTER 7

Getting into Oliver's car, I start to fish out the die when Oliver says something.

"He's here; no need to check."

"You can see him, can't you?"

"Not right now, I can't. Rose can, however."

"Oh." A minute of silence passes.

Oliver breaks the silence. "So, how did you find Tyson?"

"He found me, actually. Apparently, he used to be my dad's familiar."

"Your dad's a Keyholder?"

"He used to be, apparently."

"Oh. He got thrown out, then."

"Yeah. That's when Tyson left him."

"That makes sense. Most spirits wouldn't want anything to do with the type of people that get thrown out."

Eventually we reach the animal shelter, walk inside and start looking at the animals there.

"So, does it matter what kind of animal I'm looking at?"

"Not really, as long as you like them. Rose, keep us posted if Tyson tries to say anything." Rose responds with a nod.

"Well, let's go look at the dogs then."

Oliver stares at Rose for a moment. "Tyson is on board."

"Okay, this is bugging me. Can I just not hear her, or what's going on here?"

"Oh, yeah. If skilled enough, familiars and their owners can communicate telepathically. She doesn't like to talk in public."

After about 20 minutes of looking at dogs, I get a text. Apparently Alice got the broken door replaced. I text her back, telling her to take whatever she spent out of the money in the safe; she likely won't, but she should.

Eventually, I select a small brown dog. Not sure what breeds it's supposed to be a mix of, but he's cute and Oliver says that Rose says that Tyson says that he's okay, so it checks out. Oliver handles all of the paperwork to adopt him; with my life right now, there's no way they'd allow this if they knew what was really going on.

We take the dog and drive over to Alice's house. We set up in the living room and after an hour of guided nonsense, the dog talks.

"Ah, this is better."

"You good?"

"Yep."

"Good. Now that you can talk, I have some questions. How did my dad get kicked out of the House?"

"Oh, yeah. He tried to kill another keyholder over a rare book."

"Woah. That's..." I really can't see that... yeah, I can.

"Yeah."

Oliver hops to standing and claps. "Well, I'd better get going. I've love to stay and chat, but I've got business." Oliver says, slipping out the door.

Tyson watches him leave before launching a new subject. "So, you said you are learning Repleation right now?"

"Yeah."

"Alright. I can help you with that. Get out your book."

"Okay."

"You've gotten lucky here. I know some of this stuff from dealing with your dad."

"Cool."

As he starts teaching, Alice pokes her head in from the study.

"I don't mean to intrude, but could you-"

"Oh, sorry. Come on, let's take this over here." I head into the room I'm using, taking Tyson with me.

Tyson starts teaching me how to use Repleation properly. He's not the best teacher, but he is helping. At the very least, he's saving me from flipping back and forth through the book. A couple hours later, I'm think starting to get a handle on using the power- it's hard to test this one- when Alice pops in.

"I've got dinner ready. I've got some dog food on hand, if you need it."

"Good. I don't need much of it, but I do."

That's strange. "Why do you have dog food? You don't have a dog."

"There's this dog in the neighborhood; I keep some outside for him."

"Oh. Okay."

We head over and start eating. Alice catches me off guard by restarting a conversation from earlier today.

"So, martial arts classes. I really think they could help you."

"Really?"

Tyson jumps in. "Actually, that's not a bad idea. The House should have books on the subject, if you wanted to look there."

"Oh. I guess it could be useful... if the teachers could handle the whole super speed thing. I'll think about it."

Alice continues. "I just figure it could help you defend yourself."

"And she's right on that." Tyson says, clearly trying to pressure me into this.

"Fine. I guess it couldn't hurt."

After eating, Tyson and I head back to my book.

"Alright, enough of that power. Let's go to the next one."

"Really?"

"Yeah. They're kinda linked anyway. It should be Regeneration."

"How is that linked?"

"They are kind of opposite effects. Using Repleation slows down your body's stuff, letting you eat, drink, sleep, etc less; Regeneration speeds things way up, allowing you to recover from injury and illness rapidly."

"Okay. So-"

"Using Regeneration without Repleation to protect yourself can be dangerous; instant onset starvation is the normal result. With it, you'll just be normal hungry."

"Alright." That's one way to test Repleation; do I almost die from Regeneration? No? Then I've learned it. "How do you do it?"

"Well, like I just said, it's kind of the opposite of Repleation."

Tyson seems to be becoming better as a teacher as we continue. Maybe he's just learning how to deal with me? An hour later, he seems confident.

"Alright, now we just need to test it."

"How exactly do we do that?"

"Well, you just-"

"I think I know." I grab my bag.

As I start digging around in my bag, I pause. I really shouldn't be considering what I'm considering. It's been too long; I shouldn't start again now... No, it's fine. It's just a test. Just once should be fine... No. I can't; if I do it once, I'll do it again... But there's no other way to test it really. Or is there?

"Okay, what were you going to say?"

"To test Regeneration, you need something to heal from."

"I thought that's what you were going to say. Was kinda hoping you had a better way."

"Don't like blood?"

"Like it too much, really." I say, finding my penknife.

"Oh... Wait here." And he takes my knife and leaves the room.

A few minutes later, Alice walks into the room, holding my knife.

"So."

"Did he really need to go talk to you?"

"Seems like it. He tells me you are learning Regeneration?"

"Yeah. Sounds cool."

"Alright." She pauses for a moment before holding up my knife. "Why were you carrying this?"

"It's useful now and then. Opens packages and stuff."

"Fair. I really shouldn't do this, but... it's not mine." She sits my knife on the bed and leaves.

Alright. I guess I have to do this. It's the only way to know for sure. I'll just do it in a very different way; that's not the same thing, right? Right? Right.

I pick my knife, my hand shaking. Letting loose a breath I

didn't notice I was holding, I open the knife and run the flat of it across my palm. Don't think, just do it.

One slash later, a bit of blood runs down my palm as I close my knife and put it back into my bag. Okay, now I just need to focus. Direct my thoughts to the wound and focus. Will the skin to put itself back together.

Before my eyes, the wound closes itself and heals over. Not even a scar is left behind. That worked. So Regeneration is working. I'm not near dead from starvation, so Repleation must be working too. A snack would be good though; I've still got donuts in my bag.

As I shove donuts into my face, Tyson walks back into the room, looking... concerned, I think. Hard to tell with a dog's face.

"Did you...?"

"Yeah. It worked."

"That's good, I suppose."

"So, what's next?"

"Chapter 3, actually. Regen is the last power in chapter 2."

"It feels like I'm learning these things really fast."

"A bit fast. You've had teachers... Also, with regards to magic, legacies have power."

"Huh?"

"It's just a key phrase people use. It means the children of those who have learned magic have a natural talent to learn it themselves."

"Oh. Something valuable he gave me, I guess. About time."

"Ha. We'll start learning chapter 3 tomorrow. It's getting late."

He's right, I should go to bed. Tomorrow will be a new day. Who knows what could happen?

CHAPTER 8

I'm awoken by my phone ringing. Looking at it, I see two things of note. First, it's 7:30 in the goddamn morning; who dares call at this hour? Second, I don't know this number. Normally, I wouldn't answer, but with the ongoing situation, I really have to; it could be my dad or an ally I don't know.

"Hello? Who is this?"

"That's not important right now."

"That's the only thing that's-"

"Shut up and listen! You're making yourself powerful enemies right now by dealing with certain people. Stay out of our way or you will regret it."

"And the award for most cliched line I've ever heard goes to... this fucking bastard. Bring it or fuck off."

And I hang up and go back to sleep. Somewhere along the way, I've picked up the ability to fall asleep on command; not sure which power that is, but it's very helpful.

Waking up again, I see it's 10:00 now. Much better. It's Saturday now, so I have nothing to do today. I guess I should start by... checking if that call earlier actually happened. It's in the call log, so yeah. Should probably tell Guy- er, Oliver about that. He'd be at work today, so I'll just drop in.

"Hey, I'm gonna go talk to Oliver."

Tyson just barks in response as I leave.

Munching on more donuts, I hop on the bus over to that side of town and head to the pharmacy. He's at his normal post; excellent.

"Alexis. What brings you today?"

"Might want to speed up, long and serious stuff."

"Alright." he says, speeding up as he says it. I speed up as well; don't want to use too much of his time.

"This morning, I got a call from someone claiming I was making powerful enemies and trying to threaten me to stay out of their way."

"What'd you say to that?"

"I told them to fuck off."

"Language. Also, that's a reaction. I'd be on my guard if I was you."

"Yeah... I'm up to chapter 3 now."

"It's been, what, a week?"

"Yeah."

"You're on double time; for most people, it's one week per chapter through Basic Uses. With this mess on our hands, fast is good. Fly or die, as they say."

"Yeah. Anyway, that's it."

"Alright. I'll talk to my people and get back to you if I hear anything about your caller." And he slows back down to normal.

I leave, buying some more donuts on the way out. Thinking about it, I could go to the House and get a good breakfast for free. Walking over there, I slip inside and go looking for a dining room. Finding pancakes and bacon on the table, I just dig in. About an hour later, I finish up and leave to head back to Alice's house.

On the bus back, I start reading chapter 3. Soul Sight is the first power. Not sure what it is yet; only have the name from Tyson. It appears to be about attuning your senses to see invisible things like spirits. It's a really short section, so it's over before I reach my stop; the stopped train didn't help, delaying me by another hour.

As I get off the bus, something seems... off. Speed up. Guy at the bus stop staring at me; he's a regular here, likely getting on the bus. No big deal. Guy at the herb shop next to the bus stop looking shifty. Lowered his newspaper when the bus arrived. He's staring at me and shifting around in his bag. Got ya.

He pulls his hand out from his bag, revealing a small handgun. Great, more bullets. There's no way he'd be dumb enough to open fire here, on a public street, in broad daylight, right?

Suddenly snapping into super speed, he answers that question by firing at me. The sudden snap shot catches me off guard and hits me in the arm. Suppress the pain for now and dash into mêlée range so he can't do it again. Combining super speed and strength into one move, I swing at him with a super punch; he goes flying but kicks off a wall to turn in the air and open fire once again. This time, I'm ready and roll under the bullets. Then I jump up and try to dive kick this guy. Instead, I crash into the ground as he crashes into a wall.

Suddenly, someone from down the street shouts at the attacker.

"Drop the gun!"

The police are here already... wait, I think there is a police station on the next street over. This guy is dumb...

The gunman shoots at the cop. He's hit and goes to the ground, but there's another cop behind him who opens fire on this idiot. He somehow dodges the bullets by flying up and away.

The second cop calls for an ambulance to help the first. While he's doing that, I quickly regen away the bullet hole in my arm. The inevitable trip to the station is bad enough; let's not get dragged to the hospital over this.

After spending an hour being asked questions for which I have no useful answers, I finally leave the police station. Alice turns out to be waiting outside to pick me up.

"So..."

"Yeah, they attacked me again. Dude got away this time."

"Oh."

"On the other hand, he shot a cop, so his death warrant is signed."

From the back seat, Tyson laughs. "That's one way to look at it, I guess." Alice just sighs.

I just close my eyes and relax. Strange, I see a slight blue glow. Opening my eyes, it's gone. Closing my eyes again, it doesn't come back. I'll ask Tyson later.

"By the way," Alice says, snapping me out of my nothing, "someone used your dad's credit card at a gas station in town. The security footage looked like it was actually him, but they haven't found where he went from there yet."

"K."

"Also, Oliver called me- not sure where he got my number from, but there you go. Anyways, he said he found someone to teach you how to fight; he forgot to tell you while you were there. He'll drop by later with the details."

When we reach Alice's house, I tuck off into the room I've been using. I should really find somewhere else to stay; an apartment would be ideal. Alice is nice and all, but I have seen too much of her this week. She'd have to help me actually get something- no one would rent to a minor; I think it's the law, actually- but a quick search reveals a few that I can afford easily enough.

Tyson hops up on the bed next to me and just starts his next lesson with no prompting.

"Close your eyes."

"Huh?"

"It's time to learn Soul Sight. Close your eyes."

"Okay." I close my eyes. "Let me guess, now I start trying to focus and-"

"No, just the opposite. Relax and let the world do the work. The hidden world reveals itself to those who walk the path."

Just relax. I guess I should just see what there is to see. Breathe in, breathe out. Let the world happen. Hey, there's that blue glow again... I wonder?

"Hey, is this blue glow what I'm supposed to see?"

"Yeah. That's me. It should get clearer."

"K."

He's right. The glow is starting to coalesce into a loose sphere sitting next to me on the bed.

"Alright, I see you."

"Good. You'll want to practice this as you go about your life. It's much easier to spot a spirit who wants to be seen, so you'll need some more practice to see other spirits."

"I'll make sure to do that then... It feels like that was too easy."

"Eh, Soul Sight usually does. Once you read it once, you know it. From there, it's just practice. Try looking now."

I close my eyes and relax. Nothing is there.

"Keep them closed. Tell me when I appear."

About ten seconds later, the ball of light pops into view.

"Now."

"Alright. You've got it working for spirits who aren't trying to hide, so that's a good start."

Alright, I guess I'll start looking over the next part of the book. Oh, I think it's that telekinesis power. I was waiting for that.

CHAPTER 9

A couple of hours later, I hear a knocking at the door. As I'm listening in, Alice lets Oliver in and directs him into this room.

"So, I've found someone to teach you some combat skills."

"I know. Alice told me."

"Perfect. The first lesson is tomorrow at 10:30 in the morning. You should meet them in the front hall of the House."

"How much is-"

"Don't worry about it. She owes me a favor."

"Oh... Did you hear about the guy who attacked me today?"

"Yeah. From what I heard, you handled yourself pretty well."

"I mean, he hit me; I just healed it before anyone noticed."

"You survived; I'd call that 'pretty well,' given that you've been at this for just over a week."

"I suppose."

"The cops are looking for him, as are some spirit friends of mine. His days are numbered."

"Good."

"Good. Well, I'd better get underway... Wait. There is something I really should show you. Come on."

Following him, he leads me to a small park nearby.

"This is my favorite park. I played here as a kid all the time. So imagine my surprise when I found this."

He opens a door into a small storage shed, gesturing for me to follow him. Inside... this is the House!

"What?"

"This is my Door. You may as well use it; it's closer to you than yours right now."

"Thanks. Makes things easier."

I head back to Alice's house and sit down in the living room, cracking open Basic Uses and starting in on the next power. Tyson is asleep in the corner, so I'm on my own. Then again, I can handle myself that way.

I'm supposed to use my own inner spirit to reach out and do stuff. That sounds... tricky. I've seen it done, so you can, but how? Well, back to reading in circles all day.

By morning, I've read this whole section about twenty times. But now, it's time to talk to this combat teacher Oliver found. Oliver's door is very quick and easy to reach, so I'm there in minutes. Grabbing a bagel from a dining hall, I wait in the front hall for this guy to show up.

Right on the tick, some girl walks in, looks around and walks over to me.

"Are you Alexis?"

"Yeah. You must be the one Oliver sent."

"Yeah. Come on."

As she leads me off into the House, I find myself staring at her. She's rather tanned and clearly keeps fit; her short blond hair... I need to stop staring. Fortunately, we reach our destination as she leads me into a side room with nice chairs, directing me to sit down.

"Teaching in your palace, I take it? Given the chairs and all."

"Yeah. Saves a lot of time."

"Alright."

Taking her hand, I slip into the darkness. When the light returns, I'm standing in the middle of the a random street with...

whatever her name was; I need to ask for names more often. There are unremarkable brick buildings to the left and right stretching as high as I can see and the road runs as far as I can see in both directions.

"Let's be clear about our goals here. With the time frame we have, training you to any reasonable level of mastery is not going to happen. Instead, I'm going to be focusing on techniques that will help keep you alive and perhaps help you defeat your attacker."

"Before we get started, I actually didn't catch your name."

"Oh, right. I'm Ella. Now, let's begin."

What feels like the next few hours is spent teaching me how to properly block a punch; it's far more complicated than I expected, really. Who even knows how much time has really passed? I imagine she does, but there you go. She stops me to take a break.

"How long was all that?"

"Who knows? In the real world, it's been about a minute. In here, time is subjective anyway."

"Did you say a minute?!"

"Yeah. I've always been really good at stretching time; it's my speciality. I'm planning on spending like a week in here, which is about two- two and a half- hours outside."

I whistle in surprise. "Oh. That's one way to do it."

"So, next up: let's start throwing some punches."

Eventually, her lesson comes to an end and we return to the House. Checking my phone, it's been just over two hours... and I'm ready for bed... at like noon.

She breaks the silence. "So, what time are you available tomorrow?"

"Tomorrow? Anytime after 6 PM works... er, that's 5 PM here."

"I hate time zones. I'll be in the main room at 6 PM, House time. Bring your copy of Basic Uses; we'll need it."

And she walks away. She seems strange, but she's an effective teacher. Welp, back to Alice's place. Laying on her couch, I reopen my tab of apartments. Yep, I'm going to talk to Alice about getting one of them once she gets back.

Tyson reveals himself to be over my shoulder by speaking up.

"Looking for an apartment?"

"Yeah, Alice is nice and all, but I'd like to get out of here."

"Fair. Make sure-"

"-that pets are allowed, I know."

"So, how'd your lesson go?"

"It went well. Got another lesson tomorrow."

"Alright." He pauses, seeing an apartment on my phone. "Ooh, that one looks good."

"You're right. I'll talk to Alice about it."

Alright, enough of that. Let's go back to reading; I want to learn this power already.

"Hey." Tyson interrupts me again. "Grab that other book."

"Why?"

"Because the first power in it is easy to start and I want to teach it real quick."

"Can I learn that one? Don't I need to finish this one first?"

"No. You need Soul Sight to start learning Channeling. You've got that now. Grab the book."

"What's the power?"

"This." He barks and a puff of flame escapes his mouth.

"You can do that?"

"Yeah, I can use Channeling- that and soul powers; the ones in chapter 3 that is. Grab the book."

"Alright. Let's take this out back; just so we don't set the place on fire." I grab Binding and Channeling from my bag and head out Alice's back door.

Twenty minutes of reading and five minutes of teaching later, I've got a small wisp of flame in the palm of my hand. I have to channel energy from my connection with Tyson into energy under my control. Shaking my hand, I get rid of the flame.

"You've got it. From there, it's just practice to do better. Just keep doing it to get a feel for the flow of energy. Later, lightning will fall under your control too, but I can't help there; I never learned that one."

"Alright. I'll stay out here and practice some more."

"I'll watch from inside."

And he goes inside, peering out a window. Holding my palm in front of myself, I direct the energy to recreate the flame. Directing more energy, the small wisp grows into a baseball sized ball of flame. Pointing my palm forward away from me, the ball goes with it. Now, the book said you could push it away with... Spirit Hand. Well. Releasing my hold over the energy, it bursts outward, slightly singeing my hand. Ow. Regeneration time.

Heading back inside, I glance at Tyson and sit back down on the couch. Back to Spirit Hand... actually, this makes more sense now...

"Tyson, you clever bastard." He just laughs.

Energy is energy, and he just taught me how to channel it. My own energy is just harder to access.

"Close your eyes; you'll see better without them." Tyson idly says.

I close my eyes and see a slight blue glow on myself. That must be my energy.

"Tyson, you clever bastard!"

Before I can continue reading, Alice returns, walking in with bags from the store.

"Need help putting those away?"

"That'd be great."

We head to the kitchen and start putting her groceries away.

"So, I've been thinking."

"About?"

"I was thinking about getting an apartment. I'd need your help for the paperwork, but I'm good for the money."

"Oh... That's a good idea."

"Thanks, I have those now and then." She rolls her eyes; fair enough, that joke was bad. "I've got a place in mind for where to start. I'll show you when we finish."

After we finish putting away all the stuff, I get out my phone and show her the apartment; she copies down the address and number.

"Alright. I'll talk to them tomorrow."

"Thanks. By the way, I don't need a ride to work tomorrow; Oliver showed me a shortcut."

"K."

The next day, I slip through the House, entering through Oliver's door and exiting out mine. From there, it's a short walk to the bookstore. While I'm working, I get a strange pair of texts from Alice.

"Tyson just pooped in the toilet!"

"He flushed!"

Good boy. Eventually, my uneventful shift comes to an end and I head back to Alice's house for the hour before I've got my next lesson.

CHAPTER 10

As I sit down in the living room, Alice starts talking about the apartment.

"So, I called the landlord of that apartment you were looking at. He said he could get you in as soon as Wednesday. I found that a bit fishy- he's clearly not checking anything other than 'do you have money?'- but if you want to go there, so be it."

"That sounds like the kind of sketchy sh- crap I'm down for." Need to watch my language around her. "Let's do this."

"I'll sign the lease tomorrow. I'll need the security deposit and first month's rent to give him."

I dig in my bag and hand Alice $1,000 dollars. "That should be more than you need."

"That's... how much money do you have in there?"

"All of it. I don't use banks."

"Oh."

Let's try and show off. Pointing my hand at my bag, I try and channel my spiritual energy and pull a book out of my bag. Closing my eyes to see the flow of energy, I direct it and the book jumps out of my bag and into my hand.

"Woah! Did that just-"

"Spirit Hand. I've kinda got it working." I pause, realizing that I should actually tell Alice about my next lesson. "By the way, my next martial arts lesson is in, like, half an hour."

"Oh. Alright. Hope it goes well."

"It should. The last one fit a week into two hours."

"That's quite a feat."

When I head to the House and walk in the front hall, she's already standing there.

"Did you bring-"

"Got it here." I say, holding up Basic Uses.

"Good. Follow me."

She leads me back to the same room as last time, but the chairs are gone.

"First, a quick warm up to make sure you actually learned things yesterday."

She spends about 15 minutes drilling me on the fundamentals. High punch, block, low punch, duck, weave, kick, sidestep. Then she tosses me a stick and grabs one herself. Strike, parry, sweep, disarm. That week in her head has done me well.

"Alright, you've reached the bare minimum competence for what comes next. Where are you in Basic Uses?"

"I'm starting to figure out Spirit Hand."

"Alright, I'm going to skip ahead past it and teach you how to use Inner Spirit. It's basically Spirit Hand, but you are the thing moved. It's actually a touch easier; I don't know why it comes later."

"Alright."

After a good hour and a half of teaching, I've got that trick down. She's having me use it launch even faster punches and dodges... and a god-damn double jump, which is cool as hell but makes me want to throw up.

"Alright, you can handle yourself in a fight. We're done here."

"Okay. One thing: how much does Oliver owe you for this? I'd like to-"

"The only thing he owes me is dinner and good movie for once."

"Huh? All he said was a vague statement that you owed him a favor."

"That's a laugh. He's lucky he's cute."

"Wait. Are you and he-?" Please no.

"Only the best evil fighting couple in this House." Damn it.

"Alright. I'm going to leave quickly now."

And I leave quickly. Glad I didn't say what I was thinking in there; that would have been bad. Let's not do that. Moving on.

I rush back to Alice's house and sit down. Alice just looks at me and sighs.

"Who is she?" Damn it; she's good.

"No one..."

"Martial arts teacher?"

"No..." I sigh. "She's Oliver's girlfriend, so let's not."

"Oh. Yeah, probably shouldn't."

Eventually, the awkward passes and, later on, so too does the day.

When my alarm wakes me up on Tuesday, I rush out of the house; I'm covering for morning shift today, so I need to get there. Slipping through the House, I walk in with ten minutes to spare.

While behind the register, a guy walks in looking shifty; a lot of shifty folk come in here, but this guy seems a different kind of shifty. He starts to pull something out of his waistband, but my boss grabs him by the back of the shirt and, with the help of his son, yank him outside. After a brief pause, I hear some pained grunts and someone slam into a wall followed by someone running away. My boss and his son walk back inside, the son holding what looks like a gun, and walk back into my bosses office. Alright.

After work, I head back to Alice's house. She's sitting in the living room when I arrive.

"Hey."

"So, I went over to the apartment building and dealt with the paperwork. He actually gave me the key today; said he got it ready faster."

"So, I can just move in now?"

"I don't see why not... other than the lack of furnishings."

"We can take my bed over there and just use that."

"That works. We'll leave for that in about an hour."

Once we leave, we spend the next hour moving my bed and chair and desk and various miscellaneous furniture from my room over to my apartment and set them up there. Once we get them set up, I just flop over onto my bed and stare at the ceiling.

"You good here?"

"Yeah."

"Alright. I'm leaving a copy of the lease on the counter here."

"I'll read it later."

"If you don't mind, I'm going to leave now."

"Go."

I'm alone now... except for Tyson. Sweeping my eyes around the room, I take stock. The kitchen area has a microwave oven and fridge; how nice of them to include those. That corner over there is empty; I imagine it's meant to be a living room area. That door leads to the bathroom.

You know, I'm going to take a shower. I really need to, I haven't actually taken one in a few days; didn't want to use Alice's. Slipping off my shirt and padding, I ponder what to do next. I functionally own this place; I mean, I can't do anything, but just about anything I would actually want to do.

Okay, first order of business, clean myself. I'm starting to smell. I've got all my soaps and stuff here, so I can get everything sorted out. After I'm done here, I've got to go to the store; the kitchen is near empty right now. I've got some donuts, a bag of chips and some soda. Then... who knows? I'll make it up when I get there.

Getting out of the shower, I look at myself in the mirror. Perhaps I should actually do something with my hair instead of just brushing it flat. Perhaps a ponytail... no, twin buns; they're a bit much for me normally, but I feel like showing off today.

After doing my hair up and putting my clothes back on, I walk into the main room to see Tyson reading a book, the pages turning themselves.

"I'm going to the store. You need anything?"

"Some dog food."

"K."

I catching a bus over to the grocery store and buy everything I should need. Oh, I should actually get plates and bowls and cups and silverware and stuff. I'll get plastic and paper ones for now. After handing some cash to the cashier, I take all of this stuff back to my apartment and put it away.

Alright, next move: set up food and water for Tyson. Got bowls for that, so just fill them up.

"Your food's ready."

"K. I'll get it when I want it."

"K."

And I curl up in my bed with a book.

Some time later- I need to get a clock in here- Alice calls me.

"Yes?"

"They found your dad."

"Oh, really?" Crap, just as things were looking up.

"Yeah. The cops didn't tell me where he was. All they could tell me was that he told them not to tell me anything."

"So, he's missing intentionally."

"Don't fall all over yourself to miss him now."

"Heh."

"This is going to turn into a mess now. He's gone from missing person to abandonment of a minor. The courts are getting involved now; I'll keep you posted."

"Okay."

Great, now I have to deal with the court system. That's just great. On the other hand, he and I finally agree on something: I don't want to see him either. Good riddance... I'll likely have to see him when they force him into the courtroom for this.

An hour later, I get a text from Alice.

"At work tomorrow, get a paper from your boss saying you work there."

"Y?"

"Could be useful in court. I have a plan."

"K." Odd, but I'll do it.

After I curl up on my bed with a book I've been meaning to read for months, the next thing I really know I'm waking up and it's 9:30 in the morning. The book wasn't as good as I was told, but I finished it anyway. Did I do my homework? Nope, better knock that out real quick. Grab my laptop and just do it; bend my mind's speed to get it done in a hurry and it's over with.

Just after I finish my homework, I hear a knock on my door. Opening it, I see some guy; a rather wide fellow with not a hair on his head.

"Hello."

"Hello. I was hoping you would be here. I'm Jackson; I'm the landlord here."

"Oh, okay. Nice to meet you."

"You as well. If you need to get in touch, call me or visit my office downstairs; here's my card." He hands me a business card.

"Alright."

"Well, I'll leave you to your day." And he leaves.

Okay, before I trust that, a quick web search is in order... Okay, his story checks out; the number from the card is on the website. Let's just program that number into my phone.

Okay, what's next? Locate the laundry facilities around here; the website said they had some. Likely down in the basement. Gathering up my clothes, I hop in the elevator and head down to the bottom floor. When the doors open, the smell of chlorine rushes over me. It smells like there's a pool down here. Looking around, it appears that's because there is.

Walking over to the laundry room, I load my clothes into the washer and pull up the ad for the apartment on my phone. Alright, the pool is in the list of features, I just didn't see it. I'll have to take a look later; see if it's a good pool. Not much for swimming really, but if it's free, why not? I should get a new swimsuit; my current one is rather old.

After finishing up my laundry, I return to my apartment and get dressed for work. Neither of the doors I have are near here, so it's off to the bus stop. Perhaps I should get a car; I've got my license, but never use it. Arriving at the bookstore early, I head over to my bosses office and knock on the door.

"Come on in."

"Hello. I've got a bit of a strange request."

"What's up?"

"I'm going to be winding up in family court soon and I could use a written statement from you saying I work here."

"Oh, is that all? Not a problem." He grabs a piece of letterhead from his desk drawer and writes a message on it, finishing it with a flourish and a signature. "Here you are."

"Thank you." I take the note.

"As I said, it's not a problem. Have a good day."

And I leave his office. That went well. Sometimes I don't understand him. He seems quite rough, but he's nice to his people. I guess that makes sense, now that I think about it, but that's way things go.

After work, I head over to a clothing store nearby; I need a new swimsuit to use in that pool. It's a nightmare trying to find something that works for me, but this store usually has good stuff as long as I can avoid the staff. Looking around for about an hour, I find a nice dark blue one piece that looks like it would work.

Buying it, I slip away perfectly timed to catch a bus back over to my apartment. After a quick hello to Tyson, I step into the bathroom and put on my new swimsuit. It's not perfect, but it definitely works. Slipping normal clothes on over it, I head back to the elevator and descend to the basement.

After unlocking it with my key and looking around the room with the pool, it looks... better than I expected, actually. There isn't anyone in there right now, so this is a good time to try it. Tossing my clothes into a nearby chair along with a towel, I slip into the pool. Oh, this is nice. It's rare that I actually feel like myself, but this helps.

After a few minutes, I hear someone else walk in. Oh, well, that happens; all good things must come to an end. Looking over at them, they are... the attacker from the herb shop!

Quick movement time; jump out of the water. He starts to draw a weapon from his holster, but on raw instinct, I grab it with Spirit Hand and throw it across the room. Pointing my hand at him, I call upon Tyson's power and create a ball of flame, pushing it across the room at him. After unleashing the ball, it explodes in his face; he seems startled, but unfazed. He runs forward, flying over the pool and charging at me with a knife.

Pulling back, I swivel around him and double jump over the pool and towards the door. More open spaces favor me as someone might help... the door won't open. He's holding it closed. I'm not getting out of here. Okay, if I can't run from this fight, I'll just have to win it instead. Launch another fireball at him and close to mêlée while he is blinded by the smoke. He slashes my arm with the knife; suppress the pain, it can't help me here. Swing a punch at his face, which he blocks and counters with another slash, which I dodge and leave him overextended. Then, a sweeping kick breaks his focus so he can't fly and sends him down into the pool. Finally, a bolt of lightning into the pool finishes him off... How did I do that? I guess I learned how to do that while I wasn't looking. I can't seem to do it again, so here we are.

Okay, I need to call Oliver; he should know what to do from here... First, regen that gash on my arm, then call Oliver.

"Hey, I need your help."

"What's the problem?"

"You know that guy who shot me and then a cop? He's either knocked out or dead in front of me." I Spirit Hand him out of the pool.

"Okay, where are you?"

"Basement pool of my new apartment." I give him the address.

"I'll be there soon. Don't panic."

And he hung up. A few minutes later, I hear a knocking on the door into the pool.

"Yes?"

"It's me." Oliver. Good. I open the door. He walks over and takes a look at the guy. "I think he's alive, but just barely. Congrats on winning your first battle."

Oliver pulls some rope of nowhere and ties the guy up before doing something to him.

"I'm getting him out of here. I think the cops will be happy to see him."

"Alright. His gun's over there."

"Oh, yeah. I need to take that with me." He walks over to it and it vanishes.

"How did you do that?!"

"Oh, it's pretty advanced stuff. You can store things in your Mind Palace and retrieve them later; it's where I got the rope too."

"Oh. Okay."

"I'd best get going. Don't want anyone asking questions."

Okay, grab the nearby mop and clean up the bits of my blood on the floor. I'm done in the pool for now after that, so I dry off, put my clothes back on and head back up to my apartment. As I walk back into my apartment, I start talking to Tyson.

"Well, that guy who shot me has been dealt with."

"Really?"

"He attacked me at the pool. I put him in it and hit him with lightning."

"That's one way to do it. You got lightning working?"

"Not really; I don't know how I did that." I try doing what the book says and just get a burst of flame. "Does it make sense to you that my powers seem stronger when I actually need them, 'cause that's the way things seem to be."

"Yeah. Adrenaline can be funny like that."

"Oh... That kinda makes sense." After pausing a moment to think, I continue. "Anyway, Oliver's handling the cleanup; he knows what to do."

"Alright. I made tacos."

Rather surprising, but that works; I didn't want to cook anyway. "I didn't know you could cook, but okay."

His tacos aren't that great, but it's food and it's okay enough, so I eat them. As I do so, some of the remaining taco meat assembles itself into a taco which feeds itself to Tyson. That's actually pretty funny. After eating and taking a shower to get the chlorine out of my hair, I sit on my bed and watch videos online, analyzing various cartoons for several hours, explaining the shows to Tyson. Eventually, I have to switch over to just making Tyson watch Shaun Galaxy for the rest of the day; he's got to see it, if just so he gets it when I reference the show.

While he's watching the show, I go to read a book. Looking over my books, I realize something: I'm out of magic books to read. I've finished reading both of the books I have. I need to get a new one.

"Tyson, I'm off to the House. I'll be back."

"K."

Slipping onto a bus and over to Oliver's door, I go looking for the library, which, true to form for this House, reveals itself quickly. Rather than trying to search the room, I simply call out.

"I've finished Basic Uses of Inner Power." I put the book back onto the shelf. "What's next?"

A book falls off of a shelf. "Thank you." I pick up the book and open it. Moderate Uses of Inner Power. That works. I take the book and leave the house. Taking another bus back to my apartment, I flop over onto my bed and start reading Moderate Uses. It's a whole new brick wall. It seems to start just like Basic Uses did, with information about the mind, but it will take ages before this starts making sense.

CHAPTER 11

Speaking of ages before anything happens, a full week elapses with nothing happening. I mean, Tyson finished Shaun Galaxy ("Carnelian was The Maiden the whole time?!"), so I started having him watch Magnetism Rises. As for me, I started to get a foothold into Moderate Uses; I'm pretty sure it's trying to have me predict the future.

From the Wednesday of the pool fight, it takes until the next Thursday before anything happens. As the sun dawns on that Thursday, it actually wakes me up... at like 7:00 in the morning. I should be exhausted right now, I went to bed at 3:00... Repleation, right. Looking at my phone, I have a text from Alice.

"Call me when you get up."

Well, that's a clear instruction.

"You wanted to talk?"

"Can you make arrangements to work early tomorrow? I've got us in court tomorrow starting at 1:00."

"I can try. The other cashier owes me a favor."

"Let me know when you work it out."

"K. I'll call them now."

Hanging up, I call the other main cashier. She needed the morning off last Tuesday, so she owes me one. A quick chat later and the trade is secured. I call Alice again.

"Got it."

"That was fast."

"She was already up. She's getting ready to go to work right now."

"Oh, that works."

"Yeah. Also, I was fast? You got this into court in 9 days!"

"I have friends in family court; not my first time there by far. I'll pick you up from work tomorrow; dress for the court."

"Alright, I'll make sure to do that."

Grabbing a leash and linking it up to Tyson, I head out to explore this area; I don't spend a lot of time on this end of town, so I don't really know anything here. After an hour or so, I find a nice little pizza place out here. I'm also pretty sure I found a drug dealer, but I've got enough of those from the pharmacy.

The rest of the day passes uneventfully. I put more Magnetism Rises on for Tyson while I'm at work and pick up pizza from that shop for dinner. The next morning, I head to work in the early morning, where nothing happens. Oddly, the fact that this can be boring is comforting; if it is boring, it is normal and normal is good. Alice picks me up from the bookstore and drives us over to the courthouse. As we park, she starts to give a tutorial on being in a courtroom.

"Now, make sure you-"

"I know, don't do anything stupid."

"Not remotely how I was going to put it, but that works."

We walk into the courtroom and sit down. After a couple of minutes, the judge shows up, takes her chair and begins affairs. I just sit silently, watching the scene unfold.

"We are here today concerning the matter of Alex Mondel."

Alice chimes in, remarking upon the name. "Your honor, her preferred name is Alexis."

"Oh, very well then. First point of concern: where is Kevin Mondel? He was served summons to attend."

"It appears he does not intend to attend. He did disappear intentionally, after all."

"We will deal with his obvious contempt later. It is apparent that he has no intention of fulfilling his duty of support regarding Alexis, so we must determine who will. My understanding is that you have been serving in that capacity for the last two weeks or so?"

"Since the Monday before last, yes."

"Alright. Does she have any relatives in the area?"

"Excluding her dad, I don't know of any relatives she has at all. Her mother, Maddison Mondel, has been missing for several years and neither of them had any siblings or living parents."

Her. Right. I'd honestly forgotten about dear old Mom; she just up and left a few years back and one's heard from her since. I do wonder where she went.

"Really? None? Let me check my files." The judge looks through a folder in front of her. "Huh. You're right. I have no records of any living relatives. No uncles, no aunts, no living grandparents and I hit a dead end there."

"I do have an idea, but it's a bit obtuse."

"What's that?"

"She's actually perfectly capable of taking care of herself."

The judge seems surprised. "You're proposing emancipation, then?"

"Indeed."

"Well." The judge thinks for a moment. "I'll entertain the idea, just to see. Let's step through the issues. I suppose the first issue would be to confirm that Alexis actually wants this; she hasn't actually said anything yet here."

Alice nudges me. "Sorry, your honor; I'm not acquainted with courtrooms. It sounds like a good plan to me. I practically take care of myself already."

"For the record, how old are you?"

"17, your honor. My birthday was last month."

"Alright then. Kevin has made it quite clear that he has no desire to care for her at all, so I doubt he'd have any objections regarding it. As we've established already, no one else has any standing to object, so that's not an issue. So, the next major issue is if she can support herself. Given that Alice brought this up, I assume that isn't a concern. Are you employed?"

"Yes, your honor." I pull the paper from my boss out of my bag; this must be why she had me get it. "I've got a statement here from my boss." The bailiff takes the paper and hands it to the judge.

"I see you came prepared for this. Now, do you have somewhere to live?"

"Yes, your honor. Last week, I started renting an apartment." I hand the bailiff my copy of the lease.

"Before you ask, I'm the actual name on the lease, but she is paying all of the costs involved." Alice adds.

"Excellent." The judge quickly skims the lease. "Alright. Do you have any savings of note?"

"Your honor, I've got thousands of dollars in cash securely stored in a lockbox. I've been planning on opening a bank account once my account would be safe from my dad there."

"Perfect. I'm going go place a few phone calls to check these things." She holds up the note and lease. "The court is in recess." And she leaves the room.

Alice and I step out into the hallway.

"So, that went well."

"Did it? I can't tell."

"The mere fact that she's bothering to check means she's considering this."

"Alright. You could have warned me that you were going to do that."

"Didn't I?"

"No, you never did."

"Oh. Sorry; must have forgotten." Pretty big thing to forget. "You handled yourself really well in there."

After about an hour, the bailiff calls us back into the courtroom. A few minutes later, the judge returns to the room.

"Alright. First, regarding Kevin Mondel. I'm charging him with failure to appear and issuing a bench warrant against him in that regard. I'll deal with that further when he turns up. Second, regarding the idea of emancipation, it... while that is a rare solution, I think it may be appropriate here. This is not the 'normal' situation for such an order, but it does seem to be a good choice here. To that end, I am issuing a order of emancipation in this case. Copies can be acquired from my clerk. Court adjourned."

Alice and I leave the courtroom, grabbing a few copies of that order on the way out. As we're driving, she starts planning things.

"Okay, that went better than I ever hoped."

"Yeah. I thought that kind of process took months."

"It takes months to get that in front of the judge. We already needed to see the judge due to your dad, so it saves time. Add to that the fact that I have friends in the court system and we're clean in a hurry."

"Oh. I guess that makes sense."

"So, first order of business: the lease. Let's get that clicked over to your name. The landlord should be able to do that quickly."

"Alright."

Parking next to my apartment, we head inside and walk into

Jackson's office. After a brief chat, he cancels the old lease with Alice, handing me back my money which I immediately hand back to him as I sign the new lease myself. The only change is whose name is on the paper; I made sure of that, quickly reading the new lease and comparing it to the old one, which I memorized before, reading it on the bus.

After dealing with that, I head up to my apartment as Alice goes home. When I walk in, I see Tyson, still watching Magnetism Rises.

"How'd things go?"

"Amazing, actually. My dad didn't turn up at all. In the end, the judge decided that I don't need anyone to take care of me; I can do it myself. So, I'm on my own now."

"Oh. I didn't see that coming."

"Neither did I. Alice forgot to tell me before we left."

"Fail. At least it worked."

"Yeah."

Hearing my phone ring, I pick up a call from Oliver.

"Yes?"

"You're not going to believe this. Stop by my house." He gives me his address.

"On my way."

Catching a bus over to Alice's end of town, I head to his house. He's less than a block from the park with his door. I knock on his front door, which he opens.

"Come on in."

"What's the situation?"

He holds up a piece of paper. "Someone has put out a bounty on your head among the Evil Wizards. It's a hundred grand for whoever does you in."

"Whoa!" Suppress the panic; it can't help me.

"That guy you zapped had a note about it. The bounty was issued two weeks ago, but it was only ten grand last week. Says it's to clean up a loose end; that's a hell of price for a loose end."

"Does it say who's put a price on my head?"

"Let's see if it says..." He reads over the paper. "Kevin is the name; not familiar with that one."

"Did you say Kevin? Does it have a last name?"

"No last name, just Kevin. Why?"

"That's my dad's name." I pause for a moment for... dramatic impact, I guess. "He's put a bounty on my head?"

"Oh. Um... that's a thing."

"It's fine. I hate him too; I'll just have to defend myself."

"Well then."

"Thanks. What happened to the attacker, by the way?"

"Well, I searched him, found the note and went to take him to the police, planting his gun back on him. As I got close to the station, I dropped him nearby and walked away. Then, I called the cops from a burner phone and left them to deal with it."

"That's a plan."

"It worked, didn't it?"

"I suppose."

"So, what are you going to do about your dad?"

"I... don't know. If he's really put a bounty on me, then I think this won't end until either he is arrested or one of us is dead."

"Well, I hope it's him then."

"Me too. I'd better get home."

And so I do. Eventually, I go to bed... at 4:00 am. If I don't have to sleep much, I'll sleep when I please.

CHAPTER 12

Waking up at nine in the morning is... good. I'm fully awake; that settles it, I only need a few hours of sleep. So, I have to be on my guard; I've got a massive price on my head. Tyson seems to notice that I'm on edge.

"What's wrong?"

"Oh yeah, I didn't tell you. Turns out I'm getting attacked so much because my dad put one hundred thousand dollars on my head."

"Oh. Well, we'll just have to stop him."

"That's the plan. Just have to figure out how."

"We'll figure it out as we go."

Alright. I'm just going to hide here except when I have to go somewhere... No, that won't work. I can't just hide in fear. I have to win this somehow; there's no other option. I'm going to have to fight him.

Is there any way to prove any of his serious crimes? ... I don't think so. The only proof of the attempted murder is the testimony of a talking dog. The only proof of the bounty is a note that we can't prove has anything to do with him. All they can really tag him for is failure to appear in court; that's what, a small fine?

I either have to attack him and win or get him to attack me and get caught... He put out a bounty on me instead of just attacking me in my sleep; he doesn't want to run the risk of getting caught. He wouldn't dare attack me, so I have to attack him.

"I think I have to just find him and attack. I can't think of any other way, unless you have proof of that attempted murder you mentioned."

"Nope. I watched it happen, but that's not helpful."

"As much as I really don't want to, I think I have to go on the offensive..." Pausing for a minute, I continue. "Defending myself is one thing; attacking someone else is something else entirely."

"Well, I've got your back. Justice is a dish best served cold."

"Thank you. That means a lot... Wait, isn't that revenge?" He just shrugs in response.

How do we find him? I guess we do have just wait. Wait for him to slip up and let me find him. Just live my life as normal... new normal... and stay alive until he slips up.

With that in mind, I keep banging my head upon the wall of Moderate Uses for half an hour before making a choice. I'm basically officially an adult now, so I need to make some arrangements. First stop: that used car lot I saw while exploring.

On my way over to the lot, I see a strange sight indeed: a cat riding on someone's head... that's Erica and Simon.

"What are you doing here?" I ask.

"Oh, I just felt like seeing what your town had to offer and I knew where your Door was. Wanna hang out?"

"Sure. I'm out to buy a car right now."

"I'm in."

The two of us reach the shady looking lot. Looking around, I find a small car I rather like with $1200 written on the window. I head inside and walk up to the desk.

"Hey, can I take the black Chevy for a test drive?"

They get me the keys and I take her out; she drives well enough. I head back to their desk.

"What do you think?"

Before I can say anything, Erica speaks up. "It was alright. What do you want for it?"

"We're asking $1,200 plus fees. We can handle financing if-"

I cut them off, pulling out a stack of cash. "I'll give you $1,000 cash."

Erica remarks. "If you guys handle the fees."

The desk guy thinks for a second. "Make it $1,100 and I'll take it."

"Done."

After filling out some paperwork, they give me the keys and I leave. As we get in the car, Erica starts talking.

"So, where to now, car owner?"

"Got to open a bank account."

"Oh, that sounds boring. Want to get lunch first? I'm buying."

"Can't argue with free."

"Great. Where do you get food around here?"

"Haven't a clue on this end of town."

"We're in a car now. We can go anywhere."

"Ha ha ha." I break down laughing. She's not wrong, but she says it like its a grand revelation. "In that case, I know where we're going. There's this great fish place over on the north end."

"Let's go."

One quick drive later, we're over at the restaurant and order some food.

"So, how are things going, anyway? Still getting harassed?"

"Oh yeah, you've missed a lot. Turns out, my dad's put a bounty on my head. That's the real reason why people are trying to kill me."

"Oh."

"Yeah. They've been out of my hair for a while after I electrocuted a guy in the pool."

"Sounds like you made that bounty too dangerous to claim."

"For now. It's been raised once before, after my first couple fights."

"Well, if you need any help, give me a call. I'd hate to see you get murdered."

"How kind. I can't call you without your number, you know?"

"Asking for my number now? How forward of you." She breaks down laughing, pulls out a piece of paper and writes her phone number down. It's rather strange; all the dashes are in the wrong places and its the wrong length.

"Huh?"

"Just dial it. It'll work."

"Okay." I program it into my phone, which seems to understand it. "It's in there."

"Good. Don't be afraid to use it if you need help... or just want to hang out, really." Is... she flirting with me? I don't know.

I am spared from having to figure that out by our food arriving. This place has always been quick. We enjoy our meals as the conversation drifts to recent movies... including one coming out in a couple weeks, which we both want to see. Should I ask her to see it with me? I don't know.

After we finish eating, she pays for the meal with a stack of cash; looks like crisp bills from an ATM. Then we drive over to the bank. She stays in the car while I head inside; it's very boring.

Walking in, I request to open an account. They're rather derisive at first, but after I show them the paperwork from the court, they practically bend over to get me signed up; I feel like they get commissions for new accounts. I then deposit most of my cash into my new account and head back to the car.

"Got your private vault?"

"Yeah."

"What's next?"

"I've got to go to work actually."

"Oh, well then I'd better go then. Mind dropping me off at your Door?"

"Not a problem. It's near work anyway."

After dropping her off, I drive over to work. Parking behind the bookstore, I walk in and claim my spot behind the register. Two hours into my shift, a guy walks in and stares at me before pulling a gun from a holster. Reacting super-fast, I knock the gun out of his hand with Spirit Hand. Before I can do anything else, my boss's son has tackled him and dragged him outside. An hour after that, my boss calls me into his office.

"Have a seat." I sit down. "Alright, this is going to be a shock if I'm wrong, but I imagine you knew that fella was here to kill you?"

"Yeah. My dad has a bounty on my head. It's very complicated stuff."

"Well, my son and his friend had a chat with our idiot of the day. The guy putting down the hit- your dad, apparently- is oper- ating out of a herb shop across town."

Herb shop; that can't be a coincidence. I say the address of the shop the guy who shot a cop came out of.

"That's the place. You need help 'cleaning' things up? These folks are starting to bother me." Never thought I hear my boss say that.

"No, I can handle it myself; just knowing where he is is enough. That's what I was missing. Thank you for the offer, though."

"Very well. I'll leave you to your own devices."

After my shift ends, I head back to my apartment and start

planning. If I wait too long, he could realize I know where he is now and move. I need to strike now; it's the final battle... when did I get so dramatic?

CHAPTER 13

As I'm making my plans and calling in my allies, the sun sets on Friday and dawns on Saturday. Before leaving Saturday morning, I check with Tyson.

"Okay, I think that's everything ready. I just have to finish this. You know your part?"

"Yep."

"Good. Passwords are on the notepad; destroy it when you're done."

"Understood."

I head outside and toss the keys for my car over to Erica along with a schedule of the day's events. She's got a black wig on.

"Are you sure you don't need me to help with the attack?"

"I'm sure. Oliver's helping me with that. All I need over here is for my car to move with this schedule."

"I know, building an alibi. Seriously though, call me if you need backup; I can be there in like a minute."

"Noted."

On cue, Oliver pulls up and I hop into his car. Turns out Ella's in the back seat.

"Wasn't expecting you today."

She laughs. "I'm not missing this fight. Oliver would get himself shot if he went alone."

"Hey." Oliver responds with indignation. Rose squeaks in in his defense as well.

Oliver parks near his house. We quickly walk over to the park and slip through his door. Ella beelines for a room which turns out to be an armory. She tosses me a short staff and grabs one for herself. Handling it to understand its weight and balance, I nod. Oliver takes both staves and they vanish.

To make my alibi plan work, I need to waste some time. With that in mind, the three of us head over to a dining room and have a good meal to prepare for what's to come. When the time is right, we head back out of his door and go over to the herb shop.

Taking a deep breath, I stride in with confidence, my team standing right behind me. There is just one person in the main room; he seems to work here. Is he a threat or is he just part of their cover? He spots us and moves to rush up a set of stairs; Ella sweeps her hand, dragging him down the stairs and pinning him to the wall with a shelf.

We head up the stairs where we find a group of five people sitting around a table. There are magic books sitting on the table and a sixth chair which is empty. My dad's not here. There's a bunch of cash sitting on a table off to the side.

All five of the people at the table stand up and start grabbing weapons, spinning up to super speed. Oliver pulls out the staves from earlier and tosses them to me and Ella as we all speed up to match them. He then starts shooting bolts of lightning at the enemy. After a quick nod at Ella, I rush into the attached room where the guy from chair 6 likely is, trusting in them to keep me covered.

As I run into the room, there my dad is. He seems surprised to see me, his soulless black eyes meeting mine. With a flick of the wrist, he's holding a handgun and training it on me. With the small size of the room, I can close to mêlée and strike at his arm. He pulls back, dodging the attack, but he backs into a corner and I respond with another attack at his arm, disrupting his aim and grip.

From there, Spirit Hand removes his gun from his hand and sends it to the floor. It doesn't make noise; he's holding it with magic. Okay, I need a total overwhelming attack to break his focus so he drops the gun and can't fire it.

Pushing me back with a rush of force, he pulls the gun towards him so he can see it. He opens fire, but I can weave under and around his attacks and respond with a ball of flame, covering him in flame. In response, he flees out the window, but I vault out after him and use a double jump to kick him upwards; combining it with Spirit Hand, I launch him up to the roof of the building next door.

I land on the ground. Okay, focus. With careful movements, I execute a triple jump to get up to the top of the herb shop; from there, another triple jump gets me up to the roof with my dad. His gun is sitting on the ground outside, so he's unarmed. Correction: he just pulled a sword out of thin air. He charges to close to mêlée; as he does, I launch another fireball at him, forcing him to swerve out of the way. He moves to dodge the flames before they get there; he can clearly see things before they happen.

Evading my flames, he reaches me and swings his sword at my face. I block his sword strike with my staff. Parry and counter, opening him for a strike at the head. He is left dazed and responds with a rapid loose slash; as loose and sloppy it is, he suddenly speeds up to an even faster level of speed and I'm not prepared to prevent it, suffering a large cut across the torso.

Okay, hold it together. I use a massive burst of flame to force him to retreat, giving me time to regenerate; I can't heal it all now- no time- but close it up so I don't bleed out.

Okay, I need to go on the attack; if I let him set the pace, he will eventually win. Rushing at him at maximum speed, I strike at his sword with my staff, knocking it to the ground. He seems startled; I guess he didn't predict that. Following it up, I knock him away from the sword so he can't retrieve it. A flick of the wrist tosses his sword back through the window we came out of. Now he's unarmed.

Since I can close to mêlée safely now, I can go on an all-out attack. Laying out a forceful flurry of attacks, I push him to the edge of the building; a final kick sends him flying off the roof and down to the alley behind the building. Okay, he's flat on the ground. Jumping down after him, using Inner Hand to slow my fall a bit, I strike his head with my staff; I hear a crack and he goes limp.

Okay, don't panic, stick to the plan. I slip over to the park and into the House. A quick burst of flame destroys the staff; no evidence there. Next, regen that chest slash properly. This shirt is ruined; good thing I was planning on burning it anyway. Grabbing the replacement clothes I stowed in here, I change and burn the previous outfit; no evidence there.

A few minutes later, I get a call from Oliver.

"You okay?"

"Yeah. I'm already back at the House. You good?"

"Yep. These fools are dealt with. How's your dad?"

"Dead in an alley."

"That works. Be there in a minute."

A couple of minutes later, Oliver and Ella walk into the room and we head over to my door, slipping over to my old house. Walking inside, Erica is sitting on the couch. She tosses me my keys, waves at Oliver and Ella, winks at me and leaves, using my door to enter the House.

"Alright, that's it. Now, I just gather up some stuff here and drive back to my apartment. As far as the evidence shows, I made a couple of trips over here to gather more of my things. Tyson should have made a digital paper trail for me as well, so my movements are accounted for during all of this."

Oliver responds. "Wow. That's way more thought then I'd have put in."

"I watch a lot of crime shows, so I know how people get

106

caught."

"Well, it sounds like you thought out all the angles. I'm going to head home."

He and Ella leave. I gather up some more of my clothes, load them in my car and drive back to my apartment. As I walk in, Tyson starts up a conversation.

"Is it done?"

"Yes. You get the book ordered?"

"Of course. Took a shower too."

"Good." The neighbors would have heard that. Who would believe that a dog could do that?

I put my clothes away and get on my computer. I'm free now. They should stop attacking me now; there's no one to pay the bounty. Everything can settle down into a new normal. I can start my new life properly.

EPILOGUE

Over the next month, things settle back down. After an investigation, the cops came to the conclusion that my dad was killed by some vigilante; they apparently found evidence of his crimes while searching the herb shop, so they don't seem too worried. Obviously, they suspected me initially what with the whole "being his daughter" thing, but my alibi was bulletproof. I ordered stuff online, after all; you can't dispute that paper trail.

Turns out my dad didn't have a will; no surprise there. But what that means is, as his only living relative, I actually inherited everything he owned. Most of it isn't worth talking about much. He had a couple grand in the bank, his crappy car (which I'm going to sell off)... oh, yeah, and his house. So, I own that now. Moving back in was mildly annoying- I just left that place- but it's nice to have a building.

In the end, I did ask Erica out to see the movie... and she said yes! We went to go see it in her hometown, which turned out to be London, which explains her accent and weird phone number. Today, I'm heading on a second date with Erica. We're using the Door of a friend of hers to have dinner in Paris. As for tomorrow, who really knows; only time will tell.

Whatever it may be, for once in my life, I can't wait to see what the future holds.

Printed in Great Britain
by Amazon